Saving Emily

Saving Emily

Nicholas Read

ILLUSTRATED BY ELLEN KLEM

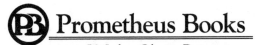 **Prometheus Books**

59 John Glenn Drive
Amherst, New York 14228-2197

Published 2001 by Prometheus Books

Inquiries should be addressed to
Prometheus Books
59 John Glenn Drive
Amherst, New York 14228–2197
VOICE: 716–691–0133, ext. 207
FAX: 716–564–2711
WWW.PROMETHEUSBOOKS.COM

05 04 03 02 01   5 4 3 2 1

Library of Congress Cataloging-in-Publication Data

Read, Nicholas, 1956–
    Saving Emily / by Nicholas Read ; illustrated by Ellen Klem.
        p. cm. — (Young readers)
    Summary: When Chris's mother remarries and they move out to the country, he feels out of place among the cattle ranchers until he meets an unusual girl who introduces him to Mr. Bridges and his animal rescue ranch.
    ISBN 1–57392–897–6 (pbk. : alk. paper)
    [1. Cattle trade—Fiction. 2. Cattle—Fiction. 3. Ranch life—Fiction. 4. Animal rescue—Fiction. 5. Individuality—Fiction.] I. Klem, Ellen, ill. II. Title. III. Young readers (Amherst, N.Y.)

PZ7.R23522 Sav 2001
[Fic]—dc21   00–051770

Printed in the United States of America on acid-free paper

For
Carolyn,
Peter,
Iris,
Walter, and Ben,
the family

Contents

Acknowledgments

I *would like to thank the many ranchers* and feedlot owners I visited in Alberta, Canada, for the valuable information they provided me. I would also like to thank my editor, Steven L. Mitchell, for his commitment to Emily's story, and to Prometheus Books for allowing me to tell it here.

Chapter One

Difficult Beginnings

*M*arigold *looked down at Emily and worried.* Of all the calves she'd had in the last twelve years, Emily was the smallest, and her birth had been the most difficult. When Marigold was young, her babies had been born almost effortlessly. Like all newborn calves, they would struggle at first to find their footing, but once they had, they were all healthy and strong.

But not Emily. Her birth had been slow and painful. Marigold knew it would be as soon as she started to feel Emily appear. In the past, Marigold's young were born outside in the pasture, but not this time. This time she stayed inside a barn and had to have help from a veterinarian.

The vet reached deep inside Marigold to grab at Emily when she wouldn't come on her own. The vet also gave Marigold a shot that made her relax, but it made her feel strange. There were other men standing around as well, men Marigold was used to seeing from time to time on the ranch, and they all were busy talking as the vet worked and struggled.

The sounds of the voices, so urgent and impatient, made Marigold feel even more nervous, and if it hadn't been for the vet, Emily might not have survived. When it was over, Marigold was exhausted—more tired and worn out than she could ever remember being. The vet was tired, too. He breathed heavily, taking in big slow breaths, but when he finally found the breath to speak, his voice changed from an angry, impatient tone to a kind one. By that time, Marigold was so busy looking after Emily that she barely noticed, but when she did, the change in the vet's voice made her feel better. Suddenly she felt a little less frightened and a little more hopeful that things would be all right.

Still she worried. Emily was such a scrawny, sticklike thing, so different from the other calves she'd had, that Marigold feared her baby might not live. Each hour that passed made her feel better, but she wouldn't take her eyes off Emily, almost believing that it was only through watching her that she stayed alive.

"Emily," Marigold said as she licked her daughter lovingly from ear to tail and hoof to head. "My little girl. I wonder what life will be like for you."

"Mama?" Emily said, looking up somewhat blindly at Marigold. "Mama?" That was all she could say for now. She was only a few hours old and very unsteady.

Emily was Marigold's twelfth calf. To people she might have looked exactly like all the others, but to Marigold she was special, like no other calf she had ever seen. But that was true of all the calves she mothered. All of them had been special to her, and each one lived in her memory every day of her life.

Her first had been a young bull named Tony. He was a strong, strapping animal right from the start, and Marigold was so proud of him when he was born. She thought he was the most beautiful thing she had ever seen. And how she had cried when he was taken away from her after their first summer together.

But that's the way it had been with most of her children. They were born; they spent the warm spring and hot summer months with her on the range, grazing and suckling; and then suddenly, when the summer turned to fall and the days got shorter, they were taken away, never to be seen again.

A few of her daughters, called heifers, remained nearby. Marigold didn't know why, but the men who had come to take away her other calves had left these behind to grow up in Marigold's view, and remain on the range with her long after they had become adult cows themselves. That delighted Marigold and she hoped this would happen to Emily, too, but Emily was so much smaller than her other daughters that she had her doubts. In any case, it would be months before she would find out.

"Emily," Marigold whispered again to the spindly newborn who finally found her way to Marigold's udder to suckle. "Please grow up to be strong. For your own sake. Please grow up to be strong."

"What?" Emily said, barely looking up. She was too hungry to listen.

"Nothing, dear," replied Marigold, looking away. "Carry on eating. I was just wishing out loud, that's all."

Two days later, Marigold and Emily were still in the barn where the birth had taken place. Marigold was grateful for that because she still felt weak, and the barn was a safe place. Emily was stronger now as well, and Marigold believed that might be because they'd been kept safe from the winter weather. Not that it was much of a barn. It had four white walls made gray and dirty by the hundreds of cows and men coming through it over the years, and it had a concrete floor on which a few heaps of straw had been strewn and then kicked away. The wooden birthing pen, in which Emily had been born, had a chipped fence, and a few of the barn's windows were badly cracked. The others were fogged up.

But Marigold didn't mind. For now, it was a good place for her and Emily to be. Emily liked feeling warm and safe by her mother, and as more time passed, she felt better. But unlike her mother, and even as weak as she was, Emily was eager to leave the barn and see what lay beyond it. She saw the same dirty walls, the same concrete floor and cracked windows, and all she felt was trapped. She didn't think she was thin or scrawny; as far as Emily was concerned, she was just fine—fine enough, at least, to want to see a little more of the world. From the moment she was born, she knew that life inside four walls was no life for her. She sensed this as soon as she started to look around. One of the windowpanes had a large hole in it, and when it was light outside, Emily liked to look through it and imagine what lay beyond the barn. "That's where I want to be," she said to herself over and over again, "Out there! And the sooner, the better."

Emily got a taste of the world outside on the third day after she was born. She was standing close to her mother, thinking about having another meal, when suddenly the door to the barn banged open and a man entered. That wasn't unusual since men had been coming in occasionally to put down hay for Marigold ever since she felt Emily coming on. But this time the man had a strange-looking gun in his hand and a white plastic tag, about the size of a playing card. He walked briskly and purposefully through the door, as if he had no time to waste. It made Emily a little nervous. Marigold, too.

"Mama...," she began to say, but the man wouldn't let her finish.

Almost without breaking his stride, he reached over to her, jerked her head toward him, held the gun and the plastic close to her ear, and then with a sudden, violent BANG!, he shot a staple through her ear and into the tag.

"Yow!" Emily yelled when the staple cut through her ear. "Oh, oh, oh," she moaned. She wasn't sure if she was more hurt or frightened, but she knew she didn't like it one bit.

The man barely noticed. He turned around and walked out of the barn as quickly as he had come in. He looked like someone who had done this many times—maybe even many thousands of times—before, and Emily's moaning didn't even make him blink. One moment he was there, and the next he was gone.

"Mama!" Emily cried, when she stopped moaning. "What was that? Why did he do that to me?"

"He gave you your tag," Marigold said, soothingly, licking Emily tenderly by her ear where it hurt. "All cows wear a tag. See, I've got one. I got it when I was first born, just like you. And so did all my other calves."

"Your other calves?" Emily asked, suddenly forgetting the pain in her ear. "You had other calves?" She had no idea. She hadn't really thought about it before, but if she had, she would have guessed she was the first.

"Yes, my other calves," Marigold replied. "You're my twelfth."

"Your twelfth?" Emily said. This was a stunning piece of news. "But what happened to the others? Where are they now?"

"Never mind about that," said Marigold, trying not to allow herself to be sad. That was hard because no matter how she tried, she couldn't forget how painful it was when she saw them for the last time. It always felt as if someone were holding onto her heart and twisting it. "The point is that they all had to get tags just like you and me. Don't you want to be like all the other calves?"

Emily looked at the tag hanging from her mother's ear, thought about the pain in her own ear, and realized that she didn't. She was barely three days old, and already she'd had a scare. It made her think, even at that tender age, that if she weren't careful, there might be other men with strange guns in their hands, and she didn't like the thought of that at all, no matter what her mother said. Something stirred in her. It was like a voice, not strong, but already determined.

"And did it hurt every time the tag was put in?" Emily asked warily.

"I expect so," Marigold said. "Cattle don't talk about it much once it's done. It's just one of the mysterious things people do to us. Besides, we have other things to think about."

"Like what?" Emily asked, afraid of the warning tone in her mother's voice, but still determined to find out.

"Never mind," Marigold said. "Don't worry about them now. For the next little while, everything will be fine. We'll be out in the pasture with all the other cows, and you'll enjoy yourself. It will get warm soon, winter will be over, and you'll like playing with the other calves out there."

"Out there." Emily repeated those magic words to herself over and over again. Except now they didn't seem quite so magical. Now they seemed a little threatening, too.

"Okay," she said quietly to Marigold. "I won't worry." She didn't know what else to say. Apart from the man with the staple gun, the only things she really knew about life were what her mother told her, and if her mother said not to worry, she supposed she shouldn't. But from then on when she looked out through the hole in the window, and felt the chilly air it let through on her face, her excitement was different. She was still eager to leave and be "out there," but she wasn't going to be just like all the other cows. Not Emily. That was something she felt as firmly as the floor beneath her hooves.

"Mama," she asked Marigold again the next day, "will you tell me now what happened to your other calves?" She had thought about it all night and was determined to find out.

Marigold didn't care. She told her to "Hush!" and not trouble herself about them anymore.

But Emily *was* troubled, and she wouldn't be put off. "Don't you see them?"

"A few of them, yes," Marigold said with a little irritation. She didn't want to talk about it, no matter what Emily said or did.

"Only a few?" Emily asked, refusing to back down. She really was curious now. After all, if her mother didn't see her other calves, the day might come when she didn't see Emily either, and Emily didn't want that. The thought made her a little fearful. "Why not all of them?" she asked. "Where are the others? Why don't you see them?"

"Didn't I tell you to hush and not worry about that?" Marigold scolded. There was more than enough time for Emily to learn the ways of the world, she decided, so there was no need to rush into explanations that would only worry her.

Emily disagreed. "Yes, all right," she replied, "but I still want to know."

"You will," Marigold said, "you will."

"When?" Emily asked again.

"Emily!" Marigold said sternly, almost to the point of shouting. This time enough was enough. Emily realized it and decided not to say anything more. But she wasn't going to give up. If she was going to be different from all the other calves, she had to find out what they were like first. And if that meant waiting and being patient for a while, she would be. But not for long.

Chapter Two

Home on the Range

"*That calf in barn two isn't much to look at,*" Mr. Lansing, the rancher who owned Marigold and Emily, said to his wife, as he took off his hat and boots in their kitchen the day Emily was born.

"No?" Mrs. Lansing replied, only half listening. She was preoccupied with trying to get a new recipe for stew right, and it wasn't working. Was it too salty or not salty enough? She couldn't decide.

"No, it's just a stick of a thing, not like the other ones from H–13," Mr. Lansing said, rubbing his sore feet. H–13 was the number on Marigold's tag. That's how Mr. Lansing and everyone who worked on his ranch identified her. The letter "H" referred to the year in which Marigold was born, and the number "13" meant she had been the thirteenth cow born in that year. Tags were always stapled into a cow's ear when the cow was just a few days old because they were the best and only way to keep track of so many animals. Emily's tag read T–39.

The tagging system was one of the many efficiencies developed over the years to make the hard work of ranching a little easier. Even so, Mr. Lansing was often very tired. He had spent so much of his life on the range in the sun that his face was lined like a road map. Mrs. Lansing said his face underlined all the years they had spent together. She worried about him, but Mr. Lansing never thought about it. He was too busy thinking about how his cattle looked because raising cattle was his livelihood.

He bred Herefords. That's what Marigold and Emily were, and all his other cattle, too. They were a breed of beef cattle with a thick, slightly curly, almost woolly hide. Mostly this hide was as brown as a chestnut, but the animals' nearly flat faces, wide stomachs, and narrow legs were white. They also had large pink noses that seemed to fill the space under their eyes, leaving no room for their mouths. There were hundreds of thousands of Hereford cattle in that part of the country, and Mr. Lansing owned thousands of them. It was prime ranching land, and his ranch was one of the biggest.

To a lot of people, even to many ranchers, all cattle looked alike. But successful ranchers like Mr. Lansing were different. They tried to pay attention to each animal, and that's why Mr. Lansing didn't like what he saw in Emily.

"I can't understand it," he said as he thought about Marigold. "She used to be so dependable, so productive. She used to turn out some really good stock. Still, she's twelve now so she might be past it. I'll have to see."

"Who's twelve?" asked Mrs. Lansing, her head in the spice cupboard.

"The mother, who else?" Mr. Lansing replied sharply. "Haven't you been listening?" He loved Mrs. Lansing, but sometimes he worried that her heart wasn't in ranching the way his was.

"Of course, dear," Mrs. Lansing said. "I always listen to you. You know that. I just need you to stop talking now, that's all."

That was a perfect example of what he meant, Mr. Lansing thought. What did she mean, "I need you to stop talking now"? He was talking about their livelihood, the very thing that put food on their table, and she didn't seem to care.

"What do you mean you need me to stop talking now?" he asked out loud. "I was talking about H–13 and her calf. Don't you want to know?"

Mrs. Lansing pulled her head out of the spice cupboard and sighed. She thought in some ways that her husband was right, that she should want to know. But the more he talked about the ranch and the longer she lived on it, the less she liked it, and the more she needed to try other things. That's where the gourmet cooking idea had come from, and the painting class before that. She also liked to listen to the opera on the radio, something Mr. Lansing had no patience for. She tried not to mind because, despite their differences, she did love him and wanted him to be happy. But she wished he would make an effort to enjoy the things she enjoyed in the same way that he wished she would take an interest in their cattle.

"Of course, I want to know," Mrs. Lansing forced herself to say. But she didn't mean it. To her, it was one more cow on what had become a seemingly endless conveyor belt of cattle that were born, fattened up, killed, and butchered with machinelike precision. If ranching was glamorous once, it wasn't anymore, Mrs. Lansing thought. Ranching was just an industry like every other industry, and even though it was the way they made their living, she didn't like how it had become their whole lives.

Fortunately, Mr. Lansing didn't say anything more. He just harrumphed and said he wanted to take a bath before dinner. Then he picked up his boots and left Mrs. Lansing on her own. She was just as glad that he did.

It hadn't always been this way. When the Lansings met, they were attracted to each other like magnets. Mrs. Lansing thought John, with his rugged cowboy good looks, was the most romantic-looking man she'd ever seen—so unlike the city types she was used to in their pressed suits and silk ties. He had country dust all over him, and he spoke slowly and thoughtfully, like a man who really knew how to court a woman. When he walked into the jewelry store where she worked to buy a new watch for himself, she was swept off her feet instantly.

Mr. Lansing had felt the same way about Sylvia. He loved how bright and charming she was, and he swore he could hear music in her voice when she spoke. She clapped when he showed her how good he was at riding horses and roping calves, and she couldn't get over how delicious the beef he cooked tasted. She was determined to learn to make it exactly the same way just to please him. And he promised that he would learn to dance. They thought theirs would be a lifetime of happiness.

But just the way the sun sets at the end of a day, it had started to set on their marriage. They still loved each other, but the differences that attracted them to each other were now becoming problems. Mrs. Lansing felt it more keenly than her husband. Not that she would do anything to hurt him, but she was growing impatient with him and his stuffy, orderly ways. It hurt her to remember that she had learned to cook beef the way he liked almost immediately, but he had never learned to dance. He couldn't understand why that mattered.

Later, Mr. Lansing's brother, Ted, joined them for dinner the way he did most evenings. He was an active partner in the ranch and took an interest in everything that happened on it. So even if Mrs. Lansing didn't care about Emily the way Mr. Lansing wished she would, Ted certainly did.

"H–13's calf isn't much to look at," he said over the dinner table to his brother. Ted had just been to see her himself and he wasn't pleased either. "Bit of a runt, ain't she?"

Mr. Lansing barely looked up from his steak and grunted. "Yep," was all he managed to say, but Ted wasn't offended. Both were men of few words.

"Gonna keep her?" Ted asked between nervous mouthfuls of the odd-tasting potatoes his sister-in-law had prepared for them. She was always trying something new, but none of the men in the family

could understand why. They liked their food plain and simple, not dolled up with the kind of fancy herbs and spices Mrs. Lansing kept using. All those strange ingredients just spoiled the taste, they thought.

"Dunno," Mr. Lansing said, washing down his steak with a big gulp of coffee. Then, frowning at the odd mocha taste in it, he added: "I'll have to see how she does on the range."

"Guess so," Ted said. There wasn't much more to say, especially not now with this bizarre dinner in front of him. It was bad enough that the potatoes tasted so strange, but what on earth had Mrs. Lansing done with the carrots? It was as if she had shellacked them with something yellow and shiny. Actually, it was more slimy than shiny. "Yech," he thought. It was a good thing she decided to leave the meat alone or he would have starved.

"Dessert?" Mrs. Lansing asked as her brother-in-law lifted his fork fearfully over one of the glazed carrot slivers she had so carefully prepared that afternoon. She watched to see if he would actually go so far as to pierce one and eat it. He didn't. She wasn't surprised. If Mr. Lansing was bad about trying new things, Ted was worse. She wouldn't have minded so much except she hadn't married Ted. But given how much she saw of him, it was as if she had.

"Mmmm," said Mr. Lansing, sitting back in his chair, his hands on his stomach. "Dessert would hit the spot." What, after all, could his wife do to a nice piece of apple pie? he wondered. That was his favorite, and it sure would go down well after a big helping of steak.

"Great," said Ted, setting down his fork beside the carrot pieces. "What is it?"

"Baklava," Mrs. Lansing said mischievously. She knew exactly what her family thought of her experiments in the kitchen, and she loved to tease them with them. "It's a Greek dessert made with thin pastry, nuts and honey. It's a new recipe I've wanted to try for a long time. Very difficult to do the first time."

"Terrific," Mr. Lansing said in the same downhearted way he always did when he was about to come face-to-face with another of his wife's unwelcome creations. He wanted apple pie. When he'd married her, she had warned him to expect a few surprises, but lately her surprises were coming every day, and that was too much.

"Great," Ted said again, his voice as low as the ground. He wanted apple pie, too. "Greek, aye? Sounds great," he lied. "Just... great."

Mrs. Lansing smiled knowingly at both of them before returning to the kitchen where she dished out two large helpings. Once they tried it, she knew they would like it. But none for herself; she was watching her weight. She liked looking pretty and she was. She had thick brown hair highlighted with blonde tints, deep brown eyes, and a gentle, wise face. Looking at her, you got the feeling she knew a lot more than she said. Mr. Lansing always found that a bit unsettling.

She bought her clothes from a boutique in a large city over a hundred miles away from the ranch because it was the only place she could find styles she liked, and she wore makeup and jewelry sometimes just to go shopping. Other ranch wives didn't. Her favorite pieces were a pair of long, glittery earrings that framed her face like sparklers. The other ranch wives thought she was stuck up because of her fussing. Mrs. Lansing knew they thought that way about her, and she wished they didn't because she wasn't trying to stand out or make them feel bad. She was just herself; but if the other wives didn't like it, that was too bad. She did what she liked. She had her own ideas about what a ranch wife should be, no matter what her husband, his family, or the rest of the town had to say.

But it was lonely being different from everyone else, especially when all Mr. Lansing wanted to do was talk about the ranch. So sometimes when Mrs. Lansing went to bed and looked out the window at the stars, she would wish for a change. She didn't know precisely what kind of a change, except that it had to be for the better. By the time Emily was born, she had been wishing for quite a long time, and she was starting to worry if it might be too late. "I hope not," she said quietly to herself as she pulled the covers up to her chin.

"What?" Mr. Lansing mumbled, as he rolled over to face her. "Did you say something?" He had his eyes closed and was barely awake.

"No, dear," Mrs. Lansing replied, "at least not anything I haven't said before."

Chapter Three

A Change of Scene

*C*hris *looked out the window and sighed.* He had been sighing a lot lately, he realized, but now that everything had been said and done, there was nothing left to do but sigh and try to look on the bright side. At least that's what his mom said he should do: think of all the fun he would have living in the country. It would be a brand-new experience, she said, and sometimes brand-new experiences were much better than old ones. Chris wasn't at all sure that he believed her even though they had been through it again and again, but it looked now as if he had no choice but to try.

"But how do you know you won't like it until you try it?" Chris's mom said six months earlier when she brought up the idea of moving. He just knew, that's all. The idea scared him. Leave the city and all his friends? Was she out of her mind?

"Because I just know I won't like it," was all he could think of to say in reply. It's true Chris had never lived in the country and therefore couldn't say for sure that he would hate it, but if he couldn't say absolutely that he would hate it, he still had a pretty good idea that he would. He was twelve, after all, so he did know a thing or two. "For one thing, I won't know anybody. I'll miss my friends."

"I know you will," his mother said soothingly as she brushed the blonde bangs off his forehead again and again. Each time she did, they fell back to where they had hung in the first place. "But you'll make new friends. And it isn't that far away. You can always visit your friends here when you come to stay with your dad."

"I know," Chris said, brushing his mother's hand away and hanging his head close to his chest, where he started to wave it from side to side. He wasn't a big kid, but he had long arms and legs. Sometimes his mom said he was "all arms and legs," whatever that meant, and he was always fidgeting. His mom said he never sat still. Even now when his whole world was coming apart, he couldn't sit quietly. It made him feel better to move.

"But it won't be the same," he whined. "I won't go to school with them anymore. I won't see them every day. They'll forget me."

"No, they won't," his mother said, rolling her big green eyes. She was an elegant-looking woman with long limbs and a mass of auburn hair. She always stood up straight. But it was her eyes that people noticed first. They were deep and inviting and drew people to her. "After all, you'll be back here all the time," she continued. "You know your dad said you would be."

"Yeah, but he didn't say how often," Chris said, looking up at his mom as defiantly as he could. Ever since his parents had divorced two years ago, he knew that the subject of his father was a sore one with his mom. And he liked to use it to his advantage when he thought it would do him some good, like the time he wanted to stay overnight at his friend, Jason's, and his father said he could but his mother said no. He and his dad had won in the end, and he hadn't forgotten that. "Is it going to be every weekend?"

"I don't know," his mother said, trying not to get upset. She was determined that even though she and Chris's dad weren't together anymore, Chris would continue to see as much of him as possible.

Despite her differences with him, he was still Chris's father, and she didn't want Chris to forget that. "You know your dad has to be away a lot on business and that might mean that a few weekends may go by when you don't see him. But you know he'll have you with him as often as he can. He wants you with him, you know that."

"Yeah, I know," Chris said. He loved his dad a lot and liked spending time with him. His dad took him to hockey games and to restaurants for burgers, and sometimes he bought him gifts even when it wasn't Chris's birthday.

"And Andrew wants you with him, too," Chris's mother said. Andrew was the man Chris's mom was going to marry. He was a doctor in a small town about a hundred and fifty miles away from the city where Chris and his mom lived, and he was the reason they had to move. Chris wasn't ever going to forgive him for that. Not in a million years.

Added to that was the fact that Chris's mom wasn't going to have the same name as him anymore. Chris's dad's last name was James, so that was Chris's last name, too: Chris James. His mom was Helene James. But when his parents split and Andrew came along, his mom announced that she wanted to change her name to his: Sinclair.

"But why?" Chris moaned when she told him. "You've been James all your life. And James is my name. It's *our* name."

"It's your father's name, and that's why it'll always be your name," Helene said, doing her best to calm him down. "But it's custom sometimes for a woman to change her name when she gets married. When I married your dad, I changed my name to James, and now that I'm marrying Andrew, I want to change it to Sinclair. It doesn't mean I won't be your mom anymore."

"But how's it going to sound?" Chris wailed. "Me named James and you named Sinclair? It's weird. It's wrong."

"It's not," Helene said. "It'll be fine, you'll see. Names don't matter that much, not the way you think they do. And besides, it'll make Andrew happy."

Hearing that made Chris madder than ever. He wasn't ever going to forgive Andrew for that, either.

"Well, if he wants to be with us so much, then why doesn't he move here?" Chris said suddenly, thinking as he did that he had hatched upon the perfect plan. Of course, he thought to himself, it's as easy as that.

"Chris, you know he can't do that," his mother replied, shaking her head. "His medical practice isn't here. He's the only doctor where he lives, so the people there depend on him. It isn't as if he can just pick up and move any time he wants."

"But we can?" Chris said. Now he was sure he had her. It was plain that his mom was all set to bend over backward to please Andrew—Andrew the doctor, Andrew the new man in her life. But what about pleasing him, her son? Wasn't he more important to her than anyone? Let her try to explain that.

"I'm not saying it won't be hard," his mom said, putting her arm around his shoulder. "I know it might be really hard at first. Things will be new and different and maybe even a little scary. They will be for me, too."

"You?" Chris asked, surprised. He hadn't considered his mom's feelings before. He assumed she didn't care where they lived as long as they were with precious Andrew.

"Yes, me," she replied. "Don't forget, I'm a city girl, too. I've never lived in the country. I don't know if I'll like it either. Andrew tells me it's not nearly as strange as I worry it will be, and he says he has a lot of friends who will want to be friends with me. But I can't help worrying if I'll want to be friends with them. Will they be interested in the things I'm interested in? Will they like the movies I like? Will they enjoy the same books I read? Will they think I'm an awful snob because I come from the city? Will I think they're a bunch of know-nothing country hicks with straw in their teeth and hayseeds in their brains?"

Chris couldn't help laughing at that. His mom chuckled, too.

"So you see, I'm just as worried as you are." She said when their giggling stopped.

"Then why are we going?" Chris asked, waving his arms and

shaking his head. Now it seemed more obvious than ever that it was a mistake. If his mother was also worried about moving, then the whole plan was ridiculous.

"Because Andrew asked me to marry him and I said yes," his mom told him. "I also said that I—that *we*—would try living in the country, for a while at least. He knows it will be strange for us and he knows we may not like it. But he did ask if we would give it a try, and I told him we would. Now can't you do the same?"

Chris sat and said nothing for a few minutes. He didn't like the idea of moving to the country any better than he did before, but maybe from what his mom was saying, it wouldn't be forever. That, at least, was something to hope for.

"You mean to say that if I—we—hate living there, we can move back to the city?" Chris asked. "Is that what Andrew said?"

"He doesn't think we will hate it there," his mom said, deflecting his question at first. "He likes it, so he hopes we'll like it, too. But yes, I suppose if we're both really unhappy there, he'll think about finding a position at a city hospital."

"Then why doesn't he save us both the trouble and just find a job here now? That way everybody will be happy." Sometimes adults were so dumb about things, Chris thought, especially when the answer was to all their problems as obvious as it was to him now.

"Chris," his mother said sternly, "I told you that we were moving to the country and that's that. The least we can do is give Andrew and the other people who live there the courtesy of a chance. Okay?"

"You mean all those people with straw in their teeth and hay-seeds in their brains?" Chris said slyly.

"Chris," his mother scolded. She wasn't laughing now.

"O . . . kay. I guess so," he said, looking down at the ground. He knew he was beaten. Then he brightened a bit remembering that moving was a whole six months away. That was almost forever. Maybe it would never come.

But it did. Here it was six months later, and Chris and his mom were busy packing up their apartment and moving all their belongings out to Andrew's house in the country—the house that soon would be known as *their* house. Chris shuddered at the thought.

He did have to admit, though, that he liked Andrew's house. That was one thing in the whole horrible plan's favor. It was an old house, built about eighty or ninety years ago, but it was big—one of the biggest in the whole town—with a porch that ran around it like a skirt. Chris had run around it the first time he saw it. The house had large rooms with high ceilings and big windows. Chris's room was huge—twice the size of the room in the apartment he shared with his mom. There was lots of room on the walls to hang his sports posters, and Andrew said he could put them wherever he liked. He also said Chris could decorate it in whatever way he chose and even paint it any color he wanted. At first, Chris wanted to paint his room black, but his mother put her foot down, no matter what Andrew said. She wasn't going to allow her son to sleep in a black room; he was not a vampire, she said. After some arguing, they compromised on purple.

The front and backyards were big, too. There were large, old trees everywhere, perfect for climbing—something Chris hadn't done in a long time—and Andrew said his new wife could build a greenhouse in the back so that she could grow her own vegetables all year long. Chris's mom had been thrilled about that. Chris thought it was okay, too, but he was really excited about the computer in Andrew's den.

"You can use it whenever you like, once you learn how to operate it," Andrew promised.

"Cool," Chris said. He was sure he could figure it out in no time.

But the town itself was another matter. Chris had been to visit four times in the last six months, and each time the town looked just as small as it had the time before. He kind of liked the buildings because they reminded him of an old Western town. He could almost imagine outlaws with guns shooting down from the rooftops

at lawmen in the streets, the way they did in old black-and-white movies. But there weren't many buildings. It was barely a town at all. There were a few streets with banks and cafes and really hokey-looking shops on them, and then a few more streets where people's houses were. There was only one movie house, and it was showing a movie Chris had seen in the city four months earlier, and only one school with only one classroom per grade. It was where Chris would begin classes in September. The thought of *that* made him sick.

Andrew could see that Chris was upset, and he did his best to point out all the good things living in the country could offer. After that, even though Chris was still not too sure about the move, he had to admit that part of it sounded okay. Maybe. There were horses everywhere, and Andrew did promise that he could learn how to ride like a cowboy if he wanted. Chris liked the sound of that. He'd never wanted to be a cowboy, but he did like animals and thought it might be fun to ride a horse.

The town was also smack in the middle of cattle country, which consisted mostly of fields. The fields were gold-colored and mainly flat, though every once in a while they would rise gently over a hill. There were hardly any trees anywhere, and overhead the sky was as blue as the color in a paintbox. Chris thought it was strange that there were so few trees, but Andrew said ranchers cut most of them down to increase the cattle's grazing area.

Surprisingly, the town where Andrew lived wasn't the smallest in the area. There were even smaller ones down the road in every direction, and they all had big grain elevators near the railroad tracks that were painted bright yellow, red, blue, or orange, almost like giant crayons standing upright on a table. Andrew said the elevators weren't used much anymore because better transportation methods made it possible for grain farmers to move their grain greater distances than they had been able to when the elevators were built. But the elevators were still an important part of the landscape and people liked them. Chris did, too.

The cattle were *everywhere*. Thousands and thousands of them:

some solid brown, some brown and white like Emily and Marigold, and some all black. They were scattered over fields as far as Chris's eye could see. Andrew said there might be a million of them in the surrounding area. "Really?" Chris said. That sounded amazing, too many to be true. "A whole million?"

"That's what people say," Andrew said from the front seat of his car, a big blue Cadillac that cruised along so quietly it was as if the motor weren't running at all. He was taking Chris and his mom on a tour of the area. "See over there? That's the Lansing ranch, one of the biggest. He has thousands of head."

"Head?" Chris asked. "Head of what?"

"Head of cattle," Andrew said, craning over his seat to point at the Lansing spread as they sped by it. "It's how people around here refer to them." Andrew was thin and studious-looking and well over six feet tall, so he was able to lean back quite far. But when he did, his glasses started to slip off his nose. He had to push them back quickly to keep them from falling off. Chris thought that was funny.

"Oh," said Chris. He'd have to remember that and a lot of other things if he were going to fit in. "So if there are so many head, I don't suppose anyone would mind if I had one for a pet."

Now it was Andrew's turn to laugh. "Well," he said, still chuckling. "I don't know about that. I've never heard of anyone keeping a cow or a bull as a pet before. But there are 4-H clubs around here where kids raise farm animals for the annual show, and then the best ones win a prize."

"What kind of prize?" Chris asked.

"Just a ribbon," Andrew replied, "but it's quite an honor just the same, and then the boy or girl who raised the cow often gets to keep the money when it's sold."

"Really? How much money?" Chris asked.

"Sometimes hundreds of dollars," Andrew crowed, "for a really good animal."

"No kidding," Chris said. He liked the sound of that. Hundreds of dollars. Wow. "But who buys the animal?"

"Other ranches or maybe the local butcher. It depends."

"The butcher? You mean they *kill* it?" Chris asked, horrified. How could anyone raise an animal as a pet and then sell it to the butcher? What were kids like around here? he wondered.

"Yes, they kill it. Don't forget that that's how a lot of people earn their living around here. They raise cattle to provide meat for us to eat. You like burgers, don't you?"

"Yeah." Chris had to admit he did.

"Well, those burgers come from their cattle."

Of course Chris knew that. He just didn't like the idea of staring at where they came from so closely. It was one thing to go to the local burger bar for one with all the trimmings; it was another to look at a half-pound patty while it was still on the hoof. What about those big brown eyes? Well, forget the 4-H idea, he thought. He'd have to figure out another way to earn money.

"And they have a rodeo here every summer," Andrew boasted. "It's a big event. Cowboys come from all around to take part. We can go as soon as you and your mom move out here."

"A rodeo?" Chris thought. Well, why not? When he'd seen them on TV, they looked kind of stupid to him—all that riding around chasing after cows and chuckwagons and things. But if he was going to be a country boy, he supposed he ought to see for himself what they were really like. Besides, his mom had told him to look on the bright side.

As time wore on, even Chris had to admit that Andrew was a pretty nice guy. At first he thought it was weird for someone other than his dad to kiss his mom. But as he got to know Andrew, he decided he could live with it. Andrew was always really gentle with his mom, and his mom said she was never happier than when she was with him and Chris. He was nice to Chris, too. He said he didn't want to take the place of Chris's dad because no one could do that, but he hoped Chris could come to think of him as something like a second dad when he had a problem or needed to talk to someone. Chris wasn't sure he could ever do that, but it was nice of Andrew to offer.

Now it was all happening. Andrew and his mom were married; Chris had quit the only school he had ever known; and the apartment he and his mom had lived in for the past two years, ever since she and his dad split up, was all but empty. Only a miracle could keep them from moving to the country now, and miracles were in pretty short supply.

"Ready, Chris?" his mom called from the corridor. There were only a few things left to take to the moving van waiting outside and then it would be time to say a last goodbye to what had been their home. Chris felt tears welling in his eyes, and his throat was all choked up. "The country," he thought, staring out the window at a view of a parking lot he soon wouldn't see again. "What am I going to do in the country?"

"Come on, Chris," his mom called again, coming into his room. "It's time to go." Then she saw the tears in his eyes and said softly: "Don't worry, son. It'll be fine. You'll see. You'll make new friends and have lots of new adventures, and in no time you'll forget that you were ever a city kid."

"You think so?" Chris asked, trying really hard not to cry. Crying definitely wasn't cool, he believed, even when you're moving away.

"To tell you the truth, honey, I don't know," his mom said. She put her arms around him and gave him a hug. "But we can try, can't we? And remember, there's something exciting about the unknown. When you step into it, you don't know what will happen to you."

"But that's exactly the problem," Chris said. He couldn't believe his mom could be so dense, especially at a time like this.

"Yes, it is," his mom said, turning him around so that he could look directly into her big green eyes. "But sometimes, honey, that's also the joy."

Chapter Four

Brand Names

*T*he big, bright world outside the barn was everything Emily hoped it would be. The sky and the land stretched forever. The firm ground made her want to run hard and kick up her hind legs, and overhead hawks and eagles swooped and soared among the clouds.

There weren't many trees but that just made everything look bigger. To Emily's new and excited eyes, it was one enormous playground. And though she was careful to stick close to her mother at first, part of her was ready to race headlong into the unknown and never stop.

"Look," she said eagerly to Marigold on their first day on the range. "Isn't it beautiful? It's so big, not like that awful cramped barn with only that small window to look through. I'm so glad to be away from there. Aren't you?"

"Yes, I suppose so," Marigold said to please Emily. But the truth was that after twelve years of grazing the same range, she no longer saw its beauty no matter how blue the sky or how sweet the grass.

She had seen too many unpleasant things happen under that blue sky—painful things that she wished she could forget—to see the view with wonder anymore. She preferred to be safe. But she wasn't going to spoil Emily's fun by saying no.

"And look at all the others. They look like me!" Emily said. "There are so many for me to play with."

"Yes," said Marigold as cheerfully as she could, "and I'm sure they'll be glad to play with you."

It was spring and the range was full of newly born brown-and-white calves and their mothers. All of them, both bulls and heifers, were still suckling milk from their mothers, but they were learning to feed on grass, too. It was fresh grass, as new as the spring, so even though it tasted a bit strange to them at first, it wasn't long before they learned to eat it hungrily. It gave them lots of energy as well. Everywhere Emily looked calves were jumping and leaping. And she wanted to jump and leap with them.

"Then go on," Marigold said, giving Emily a little nudge with her nose. "Off with you!"

Emily didn't need any more encouragement. At last she was "out there."

"Hello," the other calves said cheerily when she came running. "Who are you?"

"Emily," she said, almost breathless with joy, "I'm Emily."

"I'm Jack," said one. "I'm Josephine," said another. "I'm Oliver," said a third. "I'm Fiona," said a fourth. On and on it went. Emily couldn't begin to remember all the names, but it didn't matter. She joined in as if she had known them all her short life, and it was terrific.

While their mothers watched from a distance to see that they came to no harm, the calves chased each other round and round the range like puppies. First one would lead, then another, then another. It didn't matter because the pleasure was in the running. The sun shone bright on their faces, and for Emily, it was like heaven.

"I love it here so much," she said to Marigold when she returned for more milk and a little caress. "I'd like to stay here forever."

"Now, now," said Marigold, "no one stays anywhere forever. Not even here."

"But I'd like to," Emily insisted, "so I will."

"You will, will you?" Marigold said, indulging her. "Okay then, but you know that things change as we get older, and you might see things differently then."

"Not me," Emily said confidently. She hadn't told her mother about wanting to be different from all the other cattle because she didn't think Marigold would understand. But she knew her own mind, and when she decided something, that was that. Or so she believed. "I can't think of another place I'd like better."

Marigold nodded, deciding it was best not to say anything. After raising eleven calves, she knew how headstrong they could be. But they all learned in the end, and Emily would, too. Besides, she didn't want to spoil Emily's happiness because she knew how fleeting it might be. Events beyond her control would see to that.

Emily wasn't as naive as Marigold thought. She hadn't forgotten what the man with the tag had done to her, so she was always a little on guard. But that didn't stop her from enjoying herself. The sun continued to shine, and the games she played with the other calves were as much fun on the second, third, and fourth days as they had been on the first. She ran after her new friends, and they ran after her. They watched the birds circle and loop in the sky, and they ate and ate and ate.

Jack, the first bull she met, soon became her favorite friend. He was full of adventure and mischief, and Emily thought he was grand. He was a lot bigger and stronger than she was, but he was gentle and had an enthusiastic voice. Emily was always glad to hear it.

"Come on, Emily," he teased when a game began. "See if you can catch me today."

Emily knew he could run faster than she could, but that didn't stop her from outsmarting him. When she realized she couldn't catch him, she made him chase her, but instead of running in a straight line the way he always did, she zigzagged through the herd like a snake. It worked. She left him choking in her dust.

"How about that?" she said proudly when he finally caught up.

"Pretty clever," he had to admit. "Pretty clever."

Then as soon as they caught their breath, they ran off to do it again. Or they joined the other calves in a new game. It was never enough.

Marigold spent her days quietly eating grass and talking with the other mothers, including her own grown calves, Paige and Cinnamon. They, unlike her other offspring, had been allowed to stay on the range with her when their first summers were over.

"Luke's a good, strong bull," Marigold said to Paige about Paige's newest calf.

"Yes, he is," Paige replied. "I'm proud of him."

"You should be," Marigold continued. "He's one of the handsomest bulls on the range. One of the handsomest bulls I've ever seen, I think. I bet the men will want to keep him."

"And Julia's lovely, too," Marigold said about Cinnamon's new heifer. "So pretty and healthy."

"I think so, too," Cinnamon said. "I hope the men will want to keep her."

"I'm sure they will," Marigold said as encouragingly as she could. "The men would be fools to part with her. Anyone can see that." Then she added with a sigh: "But I'm not so sure about Emily. She's still so small compared to the others."

Paige and Cinnamon had been mothers long enough to know that Marigold was right. Compared to the other calves, Emily was a runt. She was just so small. But they didn't like to say so. They knew from experience that it was better not to say anything. They all knew the trouble with the future was that it wasn't theirs to decide. It was up to the men, and no amount of wishing was going to change that. All they could do was wait and hope.

"It's almost summer," Paige said after a while, enjoying the warm late spring sun on her face. She sensed that Marigold and Cinnamon might be thinking the same thing, and decided she ought to say something. "I guess that means that soon..."

"Yes," Marigold interrupted. She didn't want Paige to say any more. "Yes, soon," was all she added.

"Soon," Cinnamon echoed softly. They all knew what was coming, and talking about it wasn't going to stop it.

A week later Marigold felt slightly ill waking up. The day was just like any other—the sky was blue and the sun was hot—but she sensed as soon as she opened her eyes that today would be different. There was no putting it off.

"Emily," she said firmly as her calf bent down toward her udder. "Listen to me, okay. I just want to say that whatever happens today, try not to be afraid because it will be over soon."

"What will be over soon?" Emily asked. It was no good trying not to be afraid now, not after a warning like that. "Why shouldn't I be afraid?" she asked nervously. "What's going to happen?"

"Something that happens every year at this time," Marigold replied as calmly as she could. "But once it begins it'll be over almost right away."

"What will be over? What will be over right away?" Emily was starting to panic now. She could feel the fear building up inside her like an illness. "What are you talking about?"

At that moment, about a dozen men on horseback appeared on the horizon. The smell of them and their horses filled Emily's nostrils. The voice that first spoke to her in the barn was speaking urgently to her now, and it told her to run, and run fast.

"Emily!" Marigold called after her. "Don't run! It's easier if you just stay calm and let it happen. It's much worse for the bulls."

But there was no calming Emily now. She was too frightened. She was used to seeing one or two men ride by on horseback, but never so many at once. When they took off at full gallop into the herd, she was determined to escape them.

Bulls and heifers were running in every direction, scattering

throughout the range like paper in the wind. But the cowboys were such good riders that once they set their sights on an animal, there was nothing the terrified calf could do. When the calf zigged, the cowboys zagged, and in no time they had all the young animals heading exactly where they wanted.

Emily ran frantically down a hillside with the cowboys in hot pursuit, but she learned too late that this was just what they wanted. At the bottom of the hill was a series of connecting pens, one leading into another. Emily ran desperately into the first pen, joining dozens of other equally frightened calves all moaning and jostling for a way out. But there was none. The first pen led into a second smaller pen, which led into a third that eventually funneled the calves into a winding, narrow chute from which there was no escape. It was so narrow that once inside it, Emily couldn't even turn around.

The air over the chute was heavy with dust, fear, and a strange odor Emily couldn't recognize. She almost choked with it, but the only way for her to go was forward, following the line of calves ahead of her on its way to a place where there were yet more cowboys and the piercing sound of calves yelling at the top of their lungs.

The line of animals moved swiftly, but Emily was so scared that to her it felt like forever. What was going on up there? she wondered. What terrible thing was happening to make the calves ahead of her yell so much?

She found out as she rounded the last bend in the chute. With her head held up, she could see straight ahead as each calf in front of her was picked up and lowered onto a table where four pairs of human hands immediately set upon it. As two cowboys held the calf still, the others put something into its mouth and then jabbed it with something shiny. Then they took a long iron rod, glowing red on the end, and shoved it hard onto the animal's side. When the rod touched the calf, it made an ugly sound as it left an *L* mark on its skin. The calves yelled with pain when it happened. They also struggled hard to get away, but it was no use. The cowboys held them steadily till the job was done.

The cowboys worked quickly, almost like machines, as they branded each animal with the letter *L*, for Lansing's ranch. No sooner did they brand one calf, than they were on to another. And another and another. It filled the air with an acrid stench, like burning meat on a barbecue. All the calves had to be branded, fed a growth pill, and injected with antibiotics. The cowboys managed this by putting the animals in clamps that held them to the table. This prevented them from struggling and kicking. The male calves, or bulls, had to be castrated, too. A few of them, the ones that looked like they would be suitable for fathering more calves, were left alone, but there were always many more bulls born each season than were needed for breeding. It meant that most of the bulls had to undergo castration with a knife. And they weren't given any anesthetic to make the pain disappear.

Jack was only two calves ahead of Emily, and when he made it through the chute and onto the table, the cowboys took out a long knife to cut into the sack of skin between his hind legs. The pain was terrible and Jack yelled. But the cowboys were quick. It only took them a few minutes to finish the job and then brand him with the iron.

Emily watched in terror as it happened. She kept calling, "Jack! Jack!"

Then in no time it was her turn. Just as all the other calves had done, she tried her best to resist as the metal clamps came down on her. But it was useless. She was too small and the cowboys were too fast. In another second they were on top of her, forcing her to be still.

"No, no," she moaned, still struggling as the man with the iron came at her. "No."

But the man ignored her, just as he had all the other calves' protests. She was force-fed her growth pill, shot with antibiotics, and branded with the red-hot *L*.

For a moment, it hurt so much she thought she would faint. She didn't think anything could hurt so much. Having the ear tag stapled to her ear was just a pinprick compared to this. Then when she didn't think she could take it a minute longer, she smelled the black smoke, and was set free. Behind her, the cowboys moved on to another calf.

Back on the range, the pain was still terrible, but Emily wasn't quite so afraid. She didn't believe anything more could happen to her, at least not today, and somehow she managed to keep her footing as she looked around for Marigold. She was so confused she could barely tell up from down, but then she recognized her mother's face. It was the most welcome sight she had ever seen. As she walked toward Marigold, Emily stopped sometimes to lick the wound on her rump, but more than anything, she wanted to be beside her mother again, so her mother could make everything better.

"Oh, Emily," Marigold said when she caught up. "Oh my poor baby."

Then she leaned over to lick Emily's wound, gently and lovingly, doing her best to make the pain go away. But Marigold knew that it would take more than a mother's love to do that. Sometimes, if the cowboys burned too much of the skin, the brand never healed properly. Dirt could get inside it and it could become infected. Marigold had seen some cows with branding wounds still not healed after a year, and as she licked and licked, she really hoped that Emily's brand would heal fast.

The branding continued all day. Most of the calves were handled in the way Emily and Jack were, through the chute. But a few were done the old-fashioned way, on the ground. With lassos twirling over their heads like helicopter blades, the cowboys chased after the animals, yelling as they rode. When the men were in striking range, they threw their lassos at the running calves, catching them by the hind legs and bringing them to the ground with a sudden thud. They were so good at it they hardly ever missed.

Then when the calves were down, the cowboys leapt off their horses, held them and branded them. It was over in minutes.

Emily couldn't bear to watch.

As the days and weeks passed, Marigold tried her best to help Emily get over what had happened, but it wasn't easy. Emily had changed.

She wasn't the bright, cheerful youngster she had been before the branding. She was quieter now, and wary of everything. Whenever she heard the sound of trucks or horses in the distance, she jumped.

"Don't be frightened," Marigold said soothingly when Emily would bolt. "They'll be gone soon."

"I know," Emily said. "I'm fine." But deep inside, her little voice was telling her to be careful of everything. Men were the enemy; she knew that now. And if the other cattle on the range were stupid enough to wait for other terrible things to happen to them, Emily wasn't going to be one of them. She didn't know how she was going to break free or when, but one day she would. She was certain of it. But it was something she decided to keep to herself. She wasn't going to tell her mother or Jack because they might tell her to accept what she couldn't change, or worse, that she was crazy to even dream of it. So she kept quiet and waited for the right time.

Jack wasn't the same bull either. Now that he had been branded and castrated, and become a steer, he lost that sense of mischief that Emily had liked so much. And like Emily, he did not like being around people, cars, and horses.

"Does it still hurt?" Emily asked him a couple of weeks after it happened. They talked every day, and still played when it wasn't too hot.

"No, it's better," Jack said bravely. "It almost doesn't hurt at all anymore."

But Emily knew he was just being tough. Her wound still hurt, and she hadn't suffered nearly as much as he had.

Marigold was right, though, when she said nothing like the branding would happen again. The spring turned into summer and the days were hot and lazy. The calves ate more and more, and grew larger and larger. By the middle of the summer, some of the heifers weighed as much as 400 or 500 pounds. The steers weighed more than that. They were all growing into big, sturdy animals nearly the size of their mothers. All except Emily. She remained small for her age, no matter how much she ate and drank, and that continued to worry Marigold.

Runts hardly ever stayed on the range once the summer was over, and the summer was nearly gone. Autumn was a relief to some of the cows because it meant cooler days and even some welcome rain. During the summer, the rain wasn't always a comfort from the heat, mainly because it came with thunder and lightning, and since most of the trees had been cut down, there was little cover to protect the animals. But instead of relief, autumn brought fear to Marigold and many of the other mothers. Much as they hated branding day, they knew there was a worse day ahead, and as the nights grew longer and the breezes cooler, that day grew closer and closer.

"Don't worry," Marigold said to Cinnamon as reassuringly as she could. "Julia's so big and healthy, I'm sure she'll stay on the range. You'll see, this will be your lucky year."

"You think so?" Cinnamon said with a flush of hope. Last year she had given birth to a bull and she hadn't been lucky then. He had been taken away as soon as the leaves had started to turn.

"I think so," Marigold said. But she didn't dare say anything to Paige because Paige's bull calf Luke had been among those cut on branding day, and that meant only one thing. When the summer was over, he would disappear.

"And Emily?" Cinnamon asked. She could see as well as Marigold how puny Emily was, and she knew that wasn't good. But she wanted to be as encouraging as possible.

"I...I dare not say," Marigold whispered. "I dare not even hope that Emily will be spared. But at the same time I can't help myself. I remember how happy I was when you were left behind."

"I know," Cinnamon said, eyeing Julia. "I know exactly what you mean."

So as the days drifted by and Emily, Jack, and the other calves grew fatter and larger, Marigold, Cinnamon, and Paige watched and waited. Summer was almost gone. There were cool breezes all the time now, and the evenings were drawing nearer every day. Some of the leaves on the few trees left standing were beginning to turn red and gold. They looked beautiful against the blue sky, but not to the cattle. To them, they were just one more reason to worry.

The day they dreaded finally arrived at the start of October. It had been a warm, dry September, so the calves had been allowed to linger on the range longer than usual—all the mothers noticed it— but now their time was up. Just as she had known branding day was upon them, Marigold knew that the worst time had come.

She looked over at Emily, who was munching some grass next to her, and whispered to her: "Remember, Emily, that your mother loves you."

"I know," Emily said. She took her mother's love for granted, the way most youngsters do.

"You won't forget?" Marigold added.

"No," Emily said, not understanding what her mother meant. Marigold always told her that she loved her, so there was no way she could forget.

"That's good," Marigold said, watching Emily's every move. "As long as you do."

Then over the horizon, an army of trucks, horses, and cowboys suddenly appeared, and in a moment Emily knew exactly why her mother had said what she had. The enemy was back.

"It's not the fire again, is it?" Emily asked, except this time she kept still. She was almost too frightened to move.

"No, it's not the fire," Marigold said. "This is something different. This is something..."

"What?" Emily asked urgently. "This is something what?"

"Just remember that your mother loves you," Marigold said again, reaching down to nuzzle Emily one last time. "Whatever happens, remember that."

"But what will happen?" Emily asked, barely able to utter a sound now.

The cowboys and horses started to approach. Not as swiftly as they had on branding day, but steadily, and Emily knew now that nothing ever got in their way. As they started to ride faster, they bore down on Emily and all the other calves, and made them run. Emily couldn't help herself. She tried to get away, but every time she tried to turn, there would be another horse and rider in her way.

"Emily!" Marigold bellowed as Emily ran off. "Remember!"

But Emily couldn't hear her. Everywhere mothers were starting to bellow as their calves were rounded up and herded away. All over the range the cows lifted their heads to the sky and moaned and moaned and moaned.

At one point, Emily thought that she could outsmart the cowboys and horses the way she had outsmarted Jack all those weeks ago. But no matter how much she swerved and lurched, the cowboys were always there to make sure she moved straight ahead.

"Jack!" she yelled when she saw him among the others. "What's happening? What are they doing to us?"

"I don't know," Jack said. "I can't stop myself from going with them."

"Neither can I," Emily said.

"Emily!" Marigold continued to call long after her baby was gone. "Emily!"

"Luke!" Paige wailed into the afternoon. He was one of the first steers herded away.

Only Cinnamon was lucky. Just as she had hoped, Julia remained with her on the range. But she knew how her mother and sister were feeling. Last year it had been her turn to lose a calf.

"Emily!" Marigold called and called.

"Luke!" Paige moaned and moaned.

Emily stood in the large fenced-in area into which she and all the other calves had been herded and looked over in Marigold's direction. She tried to make Marigold hear when she called back to her, but all the other calves and mothers were making such a noise that no one could hear anyone clearly.

"Jack," she said when she realized that Marigold was too far away to hear her anymore, "do you think we'll ever see them again?"

"I don't know," Jack said.

"Me neither," Emily replied. But now she knew what had happened to all Marigold's other calves and why her mother hadn't wanted to tell her about them. She felt sad and afraid, even more than on branding day, and she wondered how she would face whatever was going to happen to her without her mother.

It was only the little voice inside her that kept her spirits up. It promised her that bad as things looked, one day she would find a way out. She had no choice but to believe it.

Chapter Five

Ride 'Em, Cowboy

"*Looks like it'll be another fine day*," Ted Lansing said to his brother as the sun began to come up over the ranch house.

"Good thing, too," John Lansing said, looking out the window and stretching. "We've got our work cut out for us today."

"Yeah, it's work but the boys like it," Ted said heading off to the kitchen for breakfast. "You used to like it, too, when you were younger."

Mr. Lansing laughed. "Yeah, that's the key word, younger," he said. "I'm not so young anymore."

"No?" asked Ted in a kidding way. He sat down at the table. "Ain't there a piece of you that wants to get up in the saddle again? For old time's sake maybe?"

"Mmmm," Mr. Lansing sighed. Then he added in a whisper: "Maybe for old time's sake, but Sylvia"—he nodded toward the stove where Mrs. Lansing was standing with a spatula in her hand—"would kill me."

"Pardon me," Mrs. Lansing asked, bringing plates piled high with bacon and eggs to the table. Nothing escaped her. "Why would I want to kill you?"

"No reason," Mr. Lansing said, as his wife placed his breakfast in front of him. "Ted was just asking if I'd like to ride with the boys today, that's all."

"And you think I'd kill you for that?" Mrs. Lansing said, setting down a bowl of grapefruit for herself. "I wouldn't have to, John. You'd kill yourself."

"Come on, Sylvia, John used to be one of the best cowboys on the range in his day," Ted said, winking at his brother.

"Yes, Ted, he was," agreed Mrs. Lansing. "But in case you hadn't noticed, he's not a kid anymore."

"Are any of us?" Ted asked.

"Well, Ted," Mrs. Lansing said, looking at him over the rim of a steaming cup of coffee. "I sometimes wonder about you."

"Very funny," Ted replied sarcastically.

"I thought so," Mrs. Lansing said, grinning.

They ate silently for a while so the food and the conversation could digest themselves. The men were at least grateful that Mrs. Lansing had kept the breakfast basic. Unless, of course, they counted the chives in their eggs. Now what did she go and do that for? they thought.

"What's so special about today?" Mrs. Lansing asked when it looked as if they'd finished.

"Sylvia, how many times do I have to tell you?" Mr. Lansing replied with exasperation. "It's branding day. You shouldn't even have to ask. It's part of the year, like Christmas."

"Oh yes, branding day," Mrs. Lansing replied, putting plates into the sink. "Of course, I should know that. But I think your idea of Christmas is a little different from mine, John."

"Oh, Sylvia," Mr. Lansing sighed. "You know what I mean. I don't know what's come over you lately. You used to pay ranching life the respect it deserves. Now I wonder if you even like it."

"I wonder, too," Mrs. Lansing said under her breath.

"What?" Mr. Lansing asked.

"Nothing," Mrs. Lansing said. "You're right, John. Have a good day. Hope you get to burn hundreds of little calves."

"You see, there you go again," Mr. Lansing said, his voice rising with anger. "Burning calves. You know they've got to be branded. Unless they have that big *L* on their sides, people won't know they're ours. Would you want that? Would you want people stealing 'em? Besides, it doesn't hurt them. Or if it does, it's just for a second or two. They barely feel it."

"That's what you say," Mrs. Lansing replied.

"That's what he knows," Ted said. He also was getting fed up with Mrs. Lansing's whining. Talk about a broken record. "It's what everyone else knows, too."

"I know, I know," Mrs. Lansing replied. "I'm sorry." And she was, in a way. She hated it when she and John argued. It's just that she couldn't help herself sometimes. Besides, everyone told her branding didn't hurt. When she had dared to bring it up a few years ago to some women in town, they thought she was crazy.

"Why, my husband's been branding for years," Mrs. Stevens said. "He loves it. It makes him feel young again."

"Mine, too," Mrs. Mitchell said. "One year he got so excited he fell off his horse and broke his leg."

"I remember that," Mrs. Stevens replied.

"*You* remember it?" Mrs. Mitchell said. "I never heard the end of it."

They both laughed and the conversation took off in another direction.

Mrs. Lansing supposed they were right. The men on her ranch loved branding time. It was a day when they could really test their riding and roping skills, they said when she asked. And no, the cows and bulls didn't feel a thing, they promised. They all laughed when she brought up the subject years ago.

"It's part of ranch life," one cowboy explained. "That means it's part of your life now."

And it was. Mr. Lansing was right when he said it marked the ranch calendar, and Mrs. Lansing had to admit that it was an astonishing display of a cowboy's skill. When she married Mr. Lansing and went off to watch it the first time, she was amazed at how expertly everyone rode, and how fearlessly the cowboys went after the heifers and bulls. She liked riding horses herself—it was one of the reasons she thought she would like living in the country—but she could never attempt anything as daring. She wasn't nearly good enough.

But she didn't like the violence of it: The hot irons, the burning, the castrations done without protective medicine or something to ease the pain, the way a veterinarian would use for a dog or cat. She thought it had to hurt the animals, no matter what everyone told her.

At the end of the first day, Mr. Lansing boasted that he and his team got through nine hundred head of cattle. "The boys were great," he crowed.

"Nine hundred head," Mrs. Lansing repeated. "My, my, the boys were busy, weren't they?"

"Yeah, and they'll be at it again tomorrow and the next two days after that," Mr. Lansing said, waiting eagerly for the frosty drink his wife was uncapping for him.

"Amazing," Mrs. Lansing said, "having to burn so many animals in one day. No wonder you're tired. I know I would be."

"Not burning, branding," Mr. Lansing replied after a long, cool gulp. "You're a rancher's wife now," he said, wiping his mouth with the back of his hand. "You've gotta get used to it."

"Okay," Mrs. Lansing said, pouring her own drink into a glass. "Branding. I'll remember."

"We had to do most of the bulls today, too," Mr. Lansing continued, taking great pleasure in his cold drink. There was nothing he liked better after a day's riding.

"What do you mean?" Mrs. Lansing asked, sipping hers. "What do mean 'do' the bulls?"

"Castrate 'em," Mr. Lansing replied, pulling off his boots and wriggling his toes. "Sometimes we leave a few alone for breeding, but we didn't think much of the stock this year. None are as good as last year."

"No?" Mrs. Lansing said, rubbing the back of her neck. It was strange, but sometimes conversations like this one gave her a pain back there. She didn't know why.

"No, but they'll make pretty good money at slaughter once we fatten 'em up. They'll put a lot of weight on between now and fall."

"What happens in the fall?" Mrs. Lansing asked. Everything was new to her then.

"That's when we separate the young from their mothers. Sometimes we keep a few heifers behind as breeding stock, but mainly we move 'em off to a different pasture to fatten 'em up for sale. When they're butchered, they have to be three times the size they are when they leave their mothers. If they're not worth it, we cut our losses and sell 'em for auction now. Then whoever buys 'em can try to fatten them up or sell 'em right away for slaughter. It all depends on the calf."

"Do the mothers mind when their calves are taken away?" Mrs. Lansing asked, still rubbing her neck. For some reason, the pain was getting worse.

"I guess so, for a while," Mr. Lansing said, cracking open another cold drink. "They howl for a bit, but you get used to it. It's all part of the cycle."

"I see," Mrs. Lansing replied, but she wasn't sure that she did.

"T–39's still nothing much to look at, is she?" Mr. Lansing said to Ted in the cab of his pickup truck as they cruised around the range checking the stock. T–39 was how he referred to Emily from the number on her ear tag.

"No, not much beef there," Ted said, drawing back on a soda. It was hot that day, and even though there had been a thunderstorm the night before, it was as dry as a cracker again that afternoon. "No sense keepin' her for breedin'."

"No, I can't see that there is," Mr. Lansing said. "Too bad 'cause her mother used to be so reliable. I guess she's had it, too."

"What is she, twelve or thirteen years old?" Ted asked about Marigold.

"Thirteen," said Mr. Lansing. "No, she ain't what she used to be."

"So whaddyah think?" Ted asked. "Do we sell her? She'll fetch a few hundred bucks at auction."

"Yeah, she would."

"Or straight to the slaughterhouse?"

"Don't know," Mr. Lansing said. "We'll see what happens after we get rid of her calf."

They drove off. Marigold and Emily were just two of hundreds of cattle they checked every day, so they couldn't spend more than a few minutes thinking about them.

Mr. Lansing left his decision about what to do with Emily to the last minute. "I don't know that there's any sense in tryin' to fatten her up for slaughter," he said to Ted as they drove their pickup to where the roundup was due to begin. "She's still just a bag o' bones. We might be able to get a few hundred bucks for her at auction, but maybe not. I suppose you could take her and some of the others."

"Yeah, I could," Ted said. He liked going to the auction yard because it was a good place to meet other ranchers and catch up on the news. Then after the sale, they'd go for dinner.

"Well, I'll decide after the roundup," Mr. Lansing said.

Later that day, after the roundup was over and all the calves had been removed from their mothers, Mrs. Lansing sat on her own in the kitchen and listened to the mother cows mooing. It was a low, mournful sound that went on and on. The sound never bothered her husband or Ted even though it sometimes lasted over a week, but she found it increasingly difficult to listen to the cows bawling. Mr. Lansing had explained to her during their first year together that the cows were crying for their lost young, but he said it so casually that she thought he must be kidding.

"No," he said, "that's what they're doing. Sometimes it lasts ten

days. But you get used to it, like the guy who lives next to the railway station and can't hear the train. By tomorrow you won't hear it either."

But she did. She heard it the next day and the day after that, and every day till it stopped. She heard it every year at this time, and every year it troubled her. She didn't dare tell Mr. Lansing, because he would have thought she was crazy. Besides, when she married him, she promised herself that she would do her best to understand ranch life and be a part of it. But she hadn't succeeded. Instead of getting easier, the way Mr. Lansing said it would, it was getting harder. There were some things Mrs. Lansing thought she would never understand about the ranch no matter how many times Mr. Lansing explained them.

"It's business," he said. "It puts food on the table."

"I know," she always replied. "You're right."

But as she sat by the window listening to the cows' sad lowing fill the early evening air, she wondered why it was so difficult to accept.

Chapter Six

Rodeo Fever

After a few weeks in the country, Chris had to admit that things weren't quite as bad as he thought they would be. Andrew had let him paint his room purple—his mother said it looked like a funeral parlor—and he decorated it with all his sports posters. He even put some on the ceiling. He liked the rest of Andrew's house, too, and slowly Chris found that he no longer missed the apartment he and his mother had shared in the city.

For one thing, in Andrew's house—except Andrew insisted that Chris call it his house, too—there were two rooms with TVs in them. In the city, Chris and Helene had had only one. So when Chris wanted to watch one program and Andrew and Helene something else, no one had to flip a coin. Sometimes he and Andrew watched sports together, leaving Helene on her own.

Chris liked the big yard that surrounded the house, and Andrew and Helene promised he could get a dog soon. Chris thought that would be great. He couldn't wait. He wanted to go to the local animal shelter that afternoon. But Helene said "No, we have to wait till we come back from our vacation because no one will be around to look after the dog while we're away." Chris was disappointed, but he had to admit that she had a point.

Their vacation consisted of a weeklong trip to the mountains where the three of them camped at night and hiked during the day. Andrew and Helene kept talking about the spectacular views, which Chris got kind of bored with, but he did think it was cool being so high up and far away from civilization. In the evenings, he had his portable CD player and books to keep him company, but Andrew thought they should play games instead. Chris eventually went along with the idea because he wanted to please Andrew. But once he joined in, he found that it was fun, especially when he won.

Chris had had a few misgivings about the vacation—the idea of being away with his mom and her new husband made him feel kind of uncomfortable at first—but after a few days he had to admit that he was enjoying himself. Mainly, and surprisingly, that was because he liked Andrew. He still resented Andrew for taking him away from the city, and there was no way Andrew was ever going to take the place of his real father. No way at all. He still believed his mom and dad should have stayed married, and nothing was going to change his mind about that. But Andrew was okay. Chris liked the way he always took an interest in what Chris was doing and thinking, so Chris decided that if his mom had to go and marry someone other than his dad, it might as well be Andrew.

But Chris missed his friends in the city. He also missed having friends his own age. When he rode his bike around town, he did see other kids playing, but none of them ever asked him to join in. They hardly took any notice of him. One time he chased after a ball that had been hit out of a baseball diamond, and threw it back to the players, some of whom were his own age. But other than saying thanks, they barely acknowledged him.

"Don't worry," his mom said afterward when he told what had happened. "You'll make friends in time."

"Will I?" Chris said in disbelief. The way things were going, he wondered if he ever would.

"Of course, you will," his mother said, smiling. "You have to remember that most of the kids around here have never lived anywhere else, so they've grown up with each other. You're new so it's bound to take some time for them to get to know you. But once you start school, you'll meet all sorts of new friends. You'll see."

Maybe, but school was still six weeks away, and Chris wasn't at all sure how he felt about that. A new school? A new teacher? All those new faces staring at him? Him standing there all alone at the head of the class waiting to be introduced? The idea scared him so much that sometimes he wanted to run upstairs and hide under the covers. But he didn't want to tell his mother that—not now when she was having a few problems of her own. Problems that weren't all that different from his own.

One night he overheard her saying to Andrew that adjusting to country life wasn't as easy as she thought it would be.

"It's not that I don't like it here," she said cautiously. "I do." Although from the tone of her voice, Chris knew she wasn't telling the whole truth. "It's simply that I miss some things. When you're at work, I don't have much to do."

"But you'll find things, Helene," Andrew started to say.

"I know I will," Chris's mom interrupted. "I know that. But right now I find it a bit slow. And I miss my friends."

"Of course you do," Andrew said. "Why not invite them for a visit? You know I'd love to have them here."

"I've thought of that," his mom answered, "and I'm glad you feel that way. But I want to make friends here as well. I want to fit in. But the people here are so . . ."

"Unfriendly?" Andrew ventured.

"No, no, anything but that," his mother said, her voice starting to rise. "They're definitely very friendly. My goodness, are they friendly. Every time I go into the grocery store to buy a loaf of bread, the woman at the checkout is ready to chat about the weather for what seems like forever. And the last time I went into the drug-store, the woman behind the counter spent half an hour telling me about the corns on her mother's feet, when all I wanted was a tube of toothpaste. No, they're friendly all right. It's more that they're..." She paused again. "How do I say this?"

"Plain?" Andrew suggested. "Simple? Boring?"

"That's it!" Chris's mom erupted. Chris, who was hiding behind a door, laughed.

"Chris, is that you?" Helene called.

Chris opened the door and stepped into the room.

"Were you eavesdropping?" his mom asked. "You know that's rude."

"No," Chris said, sort of lying and sort of not. After all, he hadn't heard their whole conversation, only part of it. "All I heard was Andrew saying that you thought the people here were boring, and I thought that was funny."

His mom looked embarrassed, but Andrew had a big grin on his face, so Chris smiled, too.

"Look," Andrew said, "let's forget this now, and talk about it later. I'm sure we can work something out. Right now I have news. What if I said we were all going to the rodeo on Saturday?"

He said this with such enthusiasm, as if the rodeo were Christmas, Halloween, and the Fourth of July all rolled into one, that Chris couldn't bring himself to say what he really wanted, which was, "So what?" He knew the rodeo was something Andrew was keen to show him, and had been for a long time. But Chris wasn't all that keen to go. All those cowboys whoopin' it up with cows and horses and stuff. It sounded kind of lame to him.

His mom looked as if she agreed, but then she quickly assumed the expression she always did when she was about to say something she didn't mean, but said anyway to please the listener. Chris had seen the same look a hundred times before. "The rodeo!" she replied. "Well, well." Now she was trying to smile, too. "My, my..."

"Okay, okay, so it's not a night at the opera," Andrew said.

The opera, Chris thought. Who would want to go to the opera? Grown-ups just had no idea.

"But at least it'll be new to both of you," Andrew continued, his enthusiasm undiminished. "You've never been to a rodeo, have you?"

"No," Chris said.

"Neither have I," Helene added. "But to tell you the truth, Andy, it's not something I've ever wanted to go to before."

"Well then, it'll be an adventure," Andrew said cheerfully, as if he'd tricked them into doing something they didn't want to do. "And adventures are never boring, right?"

Chris had to laugh, but his mother just gave Andrew a look. He'd seen it a hundred times before. It meant "watch out."

Saturday was no different from any other summer's day in the country. It was baking hot. It was so hot that you couldn't go half an hour without wanting another soda, and even then it never quenched your thirst. Except for the thunderstorms that would pelt rain and hail from time to time—the kind of crash-bang, drum-concert thunderstorm that sometimes scared Emily—it was always hot and dry. No one ever worried about the rodeo being rained out. Everybody knew it would take place on schedule, and arriving that afternoon in Andrew's blue Cadillac, it looked to Chris as if the whole town had turned out to see it.

Because Andrew was the town doctor, almost everyone knew him, and people kept stopping him on his way to his seat to say hello and pass the time of day. Andrew always took time to introduce Helene and Chris, and people were always pleased to meet them, saying to Helene that she must come over for coffee one day. Helene always replied that she'd love to, and that she couldn't think of anything nicer, but Chris, remembering what he'd overheard his mom say about the people in town, wondered if she was just being polite.

"Do you really want to go, or are you just being polite?" he whispered to her.

"Shhhh!" she replied with a look that pointed daggers at him. He had his answer.

The stadium was called the Stetson, after the cowboy hat, and it was full to bursting that day. There were people on every bench right up to the top of the stands, and most of them, like the men milling around the animals in the pens down below, were dressed in cowboy gear. Chris and Helene wore shorts and T-shirts, but Andrew had a cowboy hat on, too. He said he wanted to fit in and didn't like to look as if he were putting on airs. Chris thought that was nice of him.

It was a small stadium so it held only a few hundred people, but a few hundred people was a lot in a town that size, and it wasn't often that a crowd as large as the one that had gathered today got together. It was only on special occasions like parades and fireworks displays that ranching people allowed themselves to put aside their chores and take a whole afternoon off. The rodeo was *that* kind of occasion.

Along with the usual advertisements for beer, farm equipment, pickup trucks and western clothing plastered around the rodeo ring, big, brightly colored banners hung overhead welcoming people to what turned out to be the town's seventy-seventh annual rodeo, and a big town barbecue scheduled to take place immediately thereafter. Andrew said the barbecue was just as much a tradition as the rodeo—the steaks were almost as big as states, he said—so they couldn't miss it. Chris's mom didn't say anything, but Chris said he thought it might be okay. At least he might get to meet some other kids there.

"Helene, this is John and Sylvia Lansing," Andrew said as he, Chris, and Helene sat down in their seats halfway up the stands. The Lansings, who never missed the rodeo, were sitting immediately to Helene's right. Mrs. Lansing sat right beside her. "They own one of the biggest ranches around," Andrew explained.

"Hello," Chris's mom said politely. And a bit icily, Chris thought. He didn't think she was having a very good time, and the disguise she wore to hide it was starting to wear thin. "Nice to meet you," she added a little stiffly.

"Nice to meet you, too," Mrs. Lansing said. "We heard Andrew got married and we were eager to meet his new wife, weren't we John?"

Helene couldn't help thinking she was being looked up and down like one of the Lansings' prize heifers.

"Hmmm?" Mr. Lansing asked. He was too engrossed in what was taking place on the field to pay much attention. Some cowboys were already riding around the ring, and Mr. Lansing was impatient for the action to begin.

"I said we were eager to meet Andrew's new wife," Mrs. Lansing said a little testily. "Isn't that right, John?"

"Yeah, 'course we were," Mr. Lansing said, tipping his hat and nodding his head, but not really looking at her.

"Oh, forget it, John. Go back to your cows," Mrs. Lansing said, shaking her head. He didn't hear her. "So tell me, Helene—it is Helene, isn't it?"

"Yes," Chris's mom said.

"Do you like the rodeo?"

"I can't say. I've never been to one before today. But I'm sure it's ...Andrew told me that it's..."

"It's ghastly," Mrs. Lansing said.

"I beg your pardon?" Helene replied. It sounded as if she was trying to catch her breath at the same time the words spilled out.

"I said it's ghastly," Mrs. Lansing repeated. "Awful, horrible, cruel, and violent. You'll see."

"Horrible?" Chris's mom asked. "But if it's so awful, why are you here?" For the first time, Chris thought she sounded genuinely interested.

"Because I'm expected to be here," Mrs. Lansing said. "John is a rancher and he likes it, and some of our cowboys are taking part. And because I'm his wife, I'm expected to sit here and cheer for them. But I hate it. It's just a lot of noise and violence and grown men acting like little boys. You'll see for yourself. Just watch the calf-roping event.... You'll see."

"Okay...," Chris's mom replied, a little bewildered. She hadn't expected to meet anyone like Sylvia Lansing. Certainly not at a rodeo. But *she* was interesting. "Tell me, Mrs. Lansing…"

"Sylvia," Mrs. Lansing insisted. "Call me Sylvia."

"Sylvia," Helene obliged. "I know we've only just met, and this may be a bit sudden, but I was wondering if you would like to come over for a cup of coffee one day."

"I'd love to," Mrs. Lansing answered without hesitating. "I'll even bring the coffee. A nice blend from Vienna. It's hard to get here, but I manage. I'm sure you'll like it."

"I'm sure I will," Helene said, looking cheerful for the first time since she'd left her house.

The first event of the day was steer wrestling. A calf would run out of a chute at the end of the rodeo ring, then a cowboy on horseback could chase it, jump down after it, grab it, and throw it to the ground. The cowboys were judged on how long it took them to bring the calf down. Andrew said it took a lot of skill and bravery to do, but Chris and his mom couldn't help feeling sorry for the calves. One of them left the field limping.

"See that, Andrew?" Helene said, pointing to the injured animal. "Isn't the poor thing hurt?"

"It'll recover," Andrew said. "Rodeo animals are looked after really well because without them there would be no rodeo."

"Well, that makes sense… I suppose," Helene said, although given the sorry state of the limping calf, she wasn't sure she believed him.

After the steer wrestling came the bronco busting. A horse with a cowboy on its back was jabbed in the ribs and backside with spurs and electronic prods to make it leap about wildly. The idea was for the cowboy to stay on the horse as long as possible. Some really determined cowboys managed to stay on until the horse calmed down, but usually they were thrown off to the jeers and catcalls of the crowd.

"Lazy, good-for-nothin' swine," Chris heard Mr. Lansing yell after one cowboy was thrown off almost as soon as his horse burst the gate.

Once again, Chris and his mom couldn't help rooting for the

horses. But they did it silently so no one noticed. No one except Mrs. Lansing, that is.

"I feel the same way," she whispered to Helene.

Then it was time for the calf-roping. Just as in the steer-wrestling event, a calf was stuck with an electronic prod and pushed out of a chute at the far end of the ring. Then, just as they had on the day they branded Emily, a cowboy on horseback roped the animal around its neck or legs and forced it to the ground. Then he jumped off his horse and tied the calf's feet together. One end of the rope was still tied to the rider's horse, so when everything was done right, the calf would end up lying motionless on the ground with the horse standing still not far away. The faster the cowboy did this, the better his score. The crowd cheered wildly every time a rider did it well.

But sometimes the calves were injured so badly that they couldn't get up afterward. Twice horses had moved while the rope was still around the calf's neck. It meant the calves were dragged half-strangled across the ring. Andrew said it was illegal to do that, and points would be deducted from the cowboy's score.

"Hang the cowboy," Helene said a little too loudly. "What about that poor calf? It looks like it's half dead."

"Sometimes it is," a voice behind them said. Chris looked around to see a young girl about his age sitting behind him frowning.

"Huh?" Chris grunted to the girl. She was a great-looking girl with pale white skin, bright orange hair, and lots of black makeup around her eyes. She had on a bright pink dress and black ballet slippers with green beads on the tops, and she looked different from everyone else in the stands.

"I heard your mom—she is your mom, isn't she?—say the poor calf looked half dead," the girl said. "And I said sometimes it is."

"Oh," replied Chris. He didn't know what else to say. He was too fascinated by the girl.

"Mr. Bridges says calf-roping can cause severe bruising, cuts, broken bones, and even strangulation," the girl continued, as if she were reading from a book. "Sometimes, he says, you can't see the injuries, but the animal is so badly hurt that its skin can separate from its muscle. He said he knew of one calf that was injured so seriously that the only areas where the skin was still attached were around its head, neck, legs and stomach. Isn't that awful?"

"I guess so," Chris said.

"What do you mean, you guess so?" the girl snapped. "Doesn't that make you sick?"

"I guess so," Chris said again, although the truth was that he'd only heard about half of what the girl had said. "But if you feel that way about it, why are you here?"

"Because you can't complain about something unless you see it for yourself," the girl said. "Mr. Bridges taught me that, too."

"Mr. Bridges?" Chris said. "Who's Mr. Bridges?"

"He runs the Rescue Ranch," the girl said. "I help him out there during the summer and after school during the rest of the year."

"Oh," Chris said, "what's the Rescue Ranch?"

"It's a place just out of town where Mr. Bridges keeps rescued animals—dogs and horses and cows."

"Really, cows?" Chris exclaimed. Andrew said no one kept cows as pets, but here was someone who did. "You mean he keeps them as pets? My stepfather says no one does that."

"Mr. Bridges does," the girl said, "except they're not really pets. It's just that they live on his ranch and he looks after them."

"What does he do with them?" Chris asked. He quite liked the girl in an odd way, and he didn't want to lose her attention.

"He doesn't do anything with them," the girl barked. "They're just there. They live there on the ranch, and he feeds and looks after them."

"And he doesn't kill them?" Chris asked.

"Of course he doesn't kill them." The girl rolled her eyes as if he'd said something really stupid. "That's why it's a Rescue Ranch. You don't rescue animals to kill them."

"No, I guess not," Chris said.

"So, what's your name?" the girl asked.

"Chris. What's yours?"

"Gina. My mom's the hairdresser around here. She does my hair, too. Do you like it?" She ran her fingers, whose nails she had painted silver, through it and tossed it from side to side so that it shimmered in the sun. She reminded Chris a little of a pony.

"I guess so," he replied.

"You guess so?" Gina scolded. "Is that all you ever say?"

"No," Chris said, trying hard to think of something new. "I think it looks cool. Real, um . . . real orange."

"It's called burnt amber," Gina said. "It's my new color this year. Last year I was a platinum blonde."

"Oh," Chris said. He thought only grown women colored their hair, not girls, and especially not girls in the country. Didn't his mom say they all had straw in their teeth? "So how old are you?" he asked.

"Twelve," Gina replied. "How old are you?"

"I'm twelve, too," Chris said. "I just moved here from the city."

It was a little difficult keeping up a conversation over the hoots and hollers of the crowd, but Chris and Gina leaned close to one another so they could hear.

"Poor you," Gina said. "I bet you hate it here. I'm moving to the city as soon as I'm old enough. I'm going to become an actress or a model."

"Oh." She sure seemed to have strong opinions about things, but Chris liked her just the same, and she was the first person his own age he had talked to in weeks.

"So *do* you hate it?" Gina asked.

"Do I hate what?" Chris replied.

"Do you hate living in the country?" Gina asked, rolling her eyes again in a way that seemed to say, "Boys can be so dumb sometimes."

"No. It's okay, I guess." Chris chided himself for saying "I guess" again. "My mom married my stepdad—that's him sitting next to my mom; he's the doctor here—so we had to move here to be with him."

"Hello, Gina, how are you?" Andrew said, turning around when the word *doctor* was mentioned.

"Hello, Dr. Sinclair. Fine, thanks," Gina said, but not nearly as boldly as she had been when she spoke to Chris.

"Enjoying the rodeo?" Andrew asked just as a clown came into the ring and the whole audience started to laugh.

"It's okay," Gina said.

"This is my wife, Helene," Andrew continued, urging Chris's mom to turn around and be introduced. "Helene, this is Gina," he said.

"Hello, Gina," Helene said kindly.

"And I see you've met Chris," Andrew said cheerfully.

"Yes," Gina said, "we've been talking."

"Well, say hello to your mom for me," Andrew said. Then he turned around just in time to see the clown run headfirst into a fencepost.

"You know my stepdad?" Chris asked, ignoring the clown.

"Everyone does," Gina replied. "He's the doctor."

"Oh, right," said Chris. "But why did you say you thought the rodeo was okay? You told me it was awful and that the animals get badly hurt."

"I dunno," Gina said.

"Well, don't you believe it?" Chris asked. Now it was his turn to be firm.

"Of course I do," Gina replied. "You saw those calves get dragged across the field, didn't you?"

"Yeah, but Andrew says the rodeo people look after their animals really well because without them they couldn't have a rodeo. I heard him tell my mom that."

"That's just what rodeo people say. But I know what Mr. Bridges says, and I believe him."

"You mean about the cows' insides coming apart and all that?"

"Yes."

"That did sound pretty bad."

"It is. It's awful."

"I guess so," Chris said. It really was all he could think of to say. He liked Gina, but she was starting to sound a little crazy to him. From what he saw so far, he didn't like the rodeo much either, but he didn't think it was anything to get upset about. At least not the way Gina was upset. So he decided to change the subject.

"Are you going to the barbecue later?" he asked.

"The barbecue? No way!" Gina exploded. "And eat all those dead animals? No, thank you."

"Huh?" Chris asked. Now he really thought Gina was nuts. "What dead animals?"

"It's a barbecue, right? And what do you barbecue at a barbecue? Dead animals, right?"

"You mean like burgers?" Chris asked. This was too much.

"Yes," Gina said, "like burgers. Where do you think burgers come from?"

"Well, I know where they come from . . . ," Chris began, "but . . ."

"But what?" Gina said. "They come from dead animals."

Chris didn't like this conversation one bit. It was something he'd never thought about before, and he didn't like thinking about it now. Burgers were burgers; everybody knew that. And everyone ate them without thinking where they came from. Burgers were just there, that's all. Gina, he decided, was out of her mind.

"Anyway, why did you ask?" continued Gina as the crowd roared its approval of a trick riding demonstration. "Are you going?"

"I guess so," Chris said. Then he realized what he'd said yet again, and added: "Yeah, I am. My mom and stepdad want to go, and I'm going with them."

"Well, I suppose I could go and not eat anything," Gina said, more calmly. "I mean, I suppose I could go and just eat the salad and stuff."

"Yeah, why don't you do that?" Chris said, pleased again. Gina was sounding a bit more normal now. "Are you going to meet your mom there?"

"No, she told me to come home for dinner, but I could phone and say I'm going to be with you and your family. If that's okay?"

"Sure," Chris said. "Andrew has a cell phone in his car. You can use it to call her. Can't she, Andrew?" he said, tapping Andrew's shoulder.

"Sorry," Andrew said, turning around. "What did you say?"

"Can Gina use your cell phone to call her mom and say she's coming to the barbecue with us?"

"Oh sure, of course," Andrew said, smiling at Gina. "We'd love to have you come with us, Gina. The more, the merrier. Isn't that right, Helene?"

But Helene was too busy talking with Mrs. Lansing to hear what he said. So Andrew just smiled and said "never mind." Looking at her, it occurred to both him and Chris that maybe life in the country wasn't going to be quite as boring as Helene had expected.

"So tell us more about Mr. Bridges," Helene said to Gina as they all sat down at a picnic table. The Lansings had gone home because Mr. Lansing said he had animals to attend to, but not before Mrs. Lansing promised Helene again to come around on Monday with her special Viennese coffee. Helene, Andrew, and Chris had plates of barbecued ribs with them, while Gina had potato salad and garlic bread. "Do you know him, Andrew?"

After that, there was a bit of confusion as to who should answer Helene first, but Andrew let Gina.

"He's a man who runs the Rescue Ranch, like I told Chris," Gina said. "And he's got all sorts of dogs, horses, and cows, and I help him look after them when I'm not at school. I really like doing it."

"It sounds very interesting," Helene said. "Maybe Chris would like to help out sometime. Would you, Chris?"

"Well...," Chris began. As a matter of fact, he thought it might be okay, but he hated it when his mom pushed him into things, and he wished she wouldn't.

"What do you think, Andrew? Do you know this Mr. Bridges?" Helene asked.

"Oh sure," Andrew said. "Everyone knows him. He's a real character around here. He's got some very strange attitudes about things so not everyone agrees with him, but everyone respects him. He's run that ranch for years, and as Gina says, he's a real hard worker and looks after his animals very well."

"Well, Chris, what do you say?" Helene asked.

Chris was furious now. Even though he still thought Gina was kind of weird, he had wanted to ask her if he could come to see the ranch, but now that it looked as if it were his mom's idea, he didn't know what to do. "Well...," he said again.

"We could go tomorrow," Gina said excitedly. "I always go there on Sundays because that way I can give Mr. Bridges an afternoon off once a week. Otherwise he never gets any time to himself."

"Well...," Chris said yet again. He did want to go, but he wanted it to be his idea, not his mother's.

"Oh, come on, Chris," Helene urged. "What else were you going to do?"

"Um, I thought I might work on Andrew's computer," Chris said. It sounded pathetic even to him, but it was all he could think of in such a hurry.

"Oh, you can do that any time," Helene scolded. "Why not go with Gina instead? You said you wanted to spend time with kids your own age."

"Helene, I think what Chris would really like is to make up his mind for himself, isn't that right, Chris?" Andrew said.

Yes, Chris decided, he definitely was learning to like Andrew more and more.

"Andrew!" Helene said in a tone that meant, "What gives you the right to speak to me like that?"

"Tell you what. Why don't we get something to drink?" Andrew said to Helene to calm things down. "It's still blazing out, and I'm parched. What do you think?"

"Yes, that might not be a bad idea," Helene said, still eyeing her new husband warily. "Will you kids be all right?"

"Yes, fine," Gina said.

"Good. We'll bring you back some soda," Andrew said, leading Helene away.

"So, Chris, do you want to come or not?" Gina asked when the grown-ups had gone. "I'd like it if you did."

"Well...okay," Chris said. Now that his mom was gone, he decided it was all right to admit that he did want to come along after all. But he still didn't want to sound too enthusiastic about it. "I guess I could."

"Great," Gina said. "How about if we go right after lunch? I know you'll like it. The dogs run around all over the place, and it's fun feeding the horses."

"What about the cows?" Chris asked. The idea of pet cows still surprised him.

"Oh, I like them, too," Gina said. "But they sort of keep to themselves."

"Do they have names?" Chris asked.

"Oh yes, Mr. Bridges names all his animals," Gina said. "And all the animals know their names."

"Even the cows?" Chris asked in a tone of disbelief.

"According to Mr. Bridges, they do," Gina said. "And I believe him because I've seen some of the cows come when they're called."

"No kidding," Chris said. He hadn't thought of cows being that smart before. Dogs and cats, yes, but not cows. But then he realized that before today he'd never thought of cows at all.

"No kidding," Gina echoed. "Mr. Bridges says cows are a lot brighter than people think."

Chris just shrugged his shoulders and bit into his ribs. They sure were good—juicy and dripping with barbecue sauce, just the way he liked them. He thought he could eat a ton. At least usually he could. Except today, for some reason, he wasn't as hungry as usual. He wondered why. It was strange how country life was beginning to get to him, he thought. In some ways, it wasn't turning out to be anything like what he'd expected.

Chapter Seven

Going...
Going...Gone!

*E*mily missed Marigold terribly, and if Jack hadn't stayed beside her, she didn't know what she would have done. The little voice inside her told her to be strong, but given what was happening, that was easier said than done. Now she was scared of everything— both the present and the future. Neither she nor Jack knew what was going to happen, but the sight of so many men around them convinced her that whatever it was, it couldn't be good. If she ever thought people could be trusted, she knew better now. Their shouting was bad enough, but whenever they wanted to get her or Jack to move, they would hit them with sticks. It got so that just the sound of a human voice was enough to make her jump.

Often the cowboys would pass her by and move on to other cattle, but she still couldn't relax. She knew it was only a matter of time before they would be back for her. Then they'd shout and bring a stick down on her again.

She and Jack tried to comfort one another, but they didn't know what to say. If one of them had understood what was going on, that would have helped matters a little. At least it wouldn't be such a terrible mystery. But each was as ignorant as the other. Occasionally they would try to take their minds off things by saying something about a bird flying by—the sky was cloudier now, but it was still clear enough to see birds circling against it—or mention another calf in the herd, but mainly they just stayed close, watching and waiting.

They didn't have to wait long. A day later, a truck drove up to the field gate and two cowhands got out to join the other men rounding up the calves. As soon as she saw them, Emily had a terrible feeling that they would come after her. They did. After four other calves had been loaded onto the truck, it was her turn.

"Jack!" Emily moaned when the men started to hit her and push her toward the truck. "Jack, what now?"

"Emily!" Jack called back. "Just try to stay close to me and we'll be fine. As long as we stay together, we'll be fine."

Jack tried to sound brave for both their sakes, and Emily appreciated it, but his words got lost in the wind. They couldn't stay together. The men wouldn't allow it. When the cowboys forced her into the truck, they left Jack behind. They had other plans for him.

"Jack!" Emily mooed from inside the truck. "Jack, where are you?"

"Emily!" Jack called back again, but he couldn't see her anymore. The door of the truck was closed tight and there were no windows in its trailer, only narrow slats through which the eight calves inside were supposed to breathe.

Emily thought she could hear his voice faintly, but she couldn't see him or anything else through the truck's air holes. Then its engine started to rumble and she felt the floor under her begin to move. She and the other seven calves on board were jostled back and forth as the truck lurched its way out of the field and onto a gravel road. The movement made her sick—it was unlike anything she had ever felt before—but much worse than that was the certainty lying like a stone in the pit of her stomach that it was too late to hope. Jack was gone from her forever.

"Good-bye, Jack," she whispered to herself as the truck started to pick up speed. "I'll miss you." She attempted one last look through one of the narrow air holes, but it was impossible. She would never see him again.

The truck drove for about an hour, first on very bumpy roads that forced Emily and the other calves to brace themselves against the floor to avoid falling, and then on much smoother roads where the truck went faster. The truck was traveling faster than Emily had ever gone before, so that when it swayed on the curves, she felt herself being thrown against the trailer's walls. "Whoah," she moaned to the other calves when it happened. "I think I'm going to fall."

"Me, too," said her neighbor, another Hereford heifer, but bigger than Emily. In the trailer as everywhere else, Emily was the smallest of the lot.

"I can't wait for this to end," Emily added.

"Neither can I," said her neighbor. "Except when it does, what then?"

That was a good question.

At last the truck slowed down and pulled onto a gravel road that made the trailer sway from side to side. That was unsettling for the calves, too, but soon it stopped and the rear door was opened and the ramp lowered. They could see daylight again. But they didn't know what to do. Should they climb out, or should they stay put and wait? And what were they waiting for?

They found out minutes later when the two cowhands who had forced them into the truck started driving them out of it. Once again the men shouted at them and beat them if they failed to move quickly enough. But this time most of them did. All of them, including Emily, were so glad to be out of the moving black box that they almost didn't care where they were going as long as they were outside again. In fact, it took Emily a few moments to readjust her eyes to the bright light. When she did what she saw was a maze of fences and small holding pens teeming with people and other animals. It was an auction yard where hundreds of animals were being put up for sale. Most of the animals were cattle, but there were pigs, goats, and sheep, too. There were even a few horses.

The sight of the horses made Emily especially nervous because the only time she had seen a horse before was when it was under a cowboy and running hard at her. But these horses weren't going anywhere. They were in a pen themselves. They were also in terrible condition. Their backs were swayed and their ribs stuck out like a skeleton's. They looked miserable.

The pigs looked bad, too. A couple of them had red sores on their skin, and one pig had some of her insides falling out between her legs. It was awful to see. There was also a baby goat for sale, not much bigger than a small dog. It was in a pen all by itself, which made the pen look huge. There was plenty of room for it to run around, but it barely moved. It just sat in a corner bleating and bleating.

All the cattle looked like Emily—brown and white with rough, curly hides—and they were all howling constantly. Their heads were in the air and their mouths were open, mooing and mooing and mooing.

Emily was herded into a small pen not unlike the one she had been driven into when she was separated from Marigold. Except this one was smaller, so that when she and the other calves with her in the truck were pushed into it, there was almost no room for any of them to move. There was also no food or water. Emily wasn't hungry, but she was thirsty. It had been a long, hot journey and a drink would have felt good.

"What is this place?" she asked the calf closest to her. Even though she knew there was little point in asking questions like this since none of the calves was any wiser than she was, she couldn't help herself because talking out loud made her feel better. Besides, life was becoming so strange that she couldn't help searching for explanations.

"I wish I knew," said the calf, whose name was Candy. "I'm just as mixed up as you are. And probably just as scared."

"Then you're very, very scared," said Emily. She took a deep breath. Then, recalling how Jack had tried to make her feel better, she added: "But as long as we stick together, we might be all right."

"I don't know," said Candy. "All we do is get moved from one place to another, and nothing makes any sense. So I don't know what good we can do each other."

"I don't know either," Emily admitted, "but it still seems important that we try." Except now she felt a little silly saying so.

After about two hours, during which a few buyers in cowboy hats came to look at Emily, mutter a few things, and then walk away, she and her pen mates were herded out and down a short pathway into a building where a lot of human voices were shouting. Emily was getting used to that kind of shouting now—she had heard so much of it lately—but this was louder than usual. This shouting was loud enough to fill a barn.

Two by two, the calves that had been in the pen with Emily were herded through a large door and into the room where the shouting was loudest. Emily and Candy were held back by a pair of cowhands until it was their turn to go through the door, but neither of them was in any hurry. Even so, they only had a few minutes to wait. Then with a sudden shove, they were pushed through the door and into a small ring under some bright lights where a large red-faced man, as round and jowly as a snowman, was shouting so everyone could hear him. Everything humans said was gibberish to Emily, but the man's hollering was exceptional. The auctioneer barely stopped to breathe so that all his shouting ran together in one long, loud stream of noise. When he got excited, which was almost all the time, his cheeks and jowls shook like red gelatin.

"Whoooh," Emily moaned as she looked up at him and around the room. "What now?"

On the other side of the ring more men in cowboy hats sat on rows of benches built all the way to the ceiling. Most of them were silent though. They hardly spoke at all except to mutter a few words when they raised their hands to make a bid. There was also a sign with colored lights next to the auctioneer that kept flashing the

prices of the animals in bright red. The buyers paid close attention to the sign, but Emily and Candy were bewildered by it and everything else. To them it was just one big terrifying circus.

"As long as we're together," Candy said before they went in. She had decided that under the circumstances, it was all they had to hold onto.

"Right," Emily said as bravely as she could. "As long as we're together."

But when the time came to go through the strange door, Candy froze like an icicle, so the handlers had to beat her with their canes. Emily was smarter. By now she realized that the best thing to do was not fight the men anymore, because every time she did they just hit her harder, and they always got their way.

She and Candy were only in the ring a few minutes. They only had enough time to walk around a few times while the red-faced man shouted at them and the men in the bleachers, before the men with the canes came at them again and herded them out a second pair of doors on the opposite side. This time Candy was smart enough to obey them as well.

"That was strange, wasn't it?" Candy said when they had come through the doors.

"It sure was," Emily replied. "All those people looking at us. I wonder what they were looking for."

"Beats me," said Candy. "Maybe the best thing to do is just stop wondering and let things happen."

But that's where Emily knew Candy was wrong. That's how all cows behaved, and look where it got them. No, just as she promised herself all those months ago in the birthing pen, she was going to be different. Even though she had gone along with the rest of them up to now, the day would come when she would break free. She didn't know how or when, but she was determined that she would.

"Just watch me," she whispered to herself.

"What?" said Candy.

"Nothing," Emily said. "Just talking to myself."

Then a new pair of cowboys appeared to take them down another pathway to another pen. It was a narrow enclosure full of cattle crushed together, and the only way out that Emily could see was up a rough track leading into the back of a huge box, like the one that had brought her.

It was a truck about four times longer than the truck that had transported her and Candy to the auction. More cowboys stood on or near the ramp to force cattle that didn't want to climb it. It was a tough job. Some of the cattle refused to budge, and the cowboys had to beat them again and again. Other times, animals would climb the ramp almost to the top only to back down at the last minute. When this happened, they pushed back all the animals behind them. This made the cowboys very angry, and they beat the animals even harder. Sometimes the cows were so stubborn or frightened that the cowboys climbed on the fences and kicked the cows in their heads. From where Emily and Candy were standing, it looked like everybody was crazy, and neither of them wanted any part of it.

"What do you think it is about the box that makes them run from it?" Candy asked as she stared at the truck's huge trailer.

"I don't know," Emily said, "but I know we're supposed to follow them on board, so we'll find out then."

"If we ever get there," Candy said, "and I kind of hope we don't."

"Me, too," Emily said. "Me, too."

But after a while it was their turn. Despite all the commotion, the cowboys eventually got the first animals up the ramp and through the trailer door. Once the first few cows were on board, the others were quicker to follow. If some of them balked, they were beaten and kicked till they moved. When it was Emily's turn, however, she knew better and decided to move as she was told.

The truck's trailer was made of heavy, strong steel, and all along either side of it were narrow holes like the ones in the smaller truck through which the animals were supposed to breathe. There were two floors in it, one above the other, each made of steel. There was no straw for the animals to stand on, but each floor was rough and bumpy to help them keep their footing. It was dark inside, almost too dark to see, so Emily didn't know where she was supposed to go. She knew the trailer was full of cattle—she heard them moaning above and below her—but she didn't know which direction she should turn. The cowboys made up her mind for her by pushing her down onto the trailer's lower floor. It was scary doing that because she didn't know where she was jumping. She couldn't see the bottom. Luckily, it wasn't far and she got her footing back quickly. Candy was pressed up against her. All the cows were squashed together like ketchup bottles on a supermarket shelf. They couldn't even step to the side or turn around. It was the same upstairs.

The trailer also was filthy. All the floors and walls were encrusted with dung and urine, and with so many cows crushed into one space, the problem only got worse.

"Where to now?" Emily said to Candy when she felt the engine start, and the gigantic truck began to lurch forward on its giant eighteen wheels. She didn't expect an answer, which was a good thing since Candy, as usual, didn't have one.

Once again, they didn't travel too long, just a couple of hours. Nevertheless it was long enough for Emily to feel miserable and wonder if she would ever be allowed out of this dark, smelly, terrifying contraption again. Just as in the auction yard, there was no food or water, and Emily was very thirsty. In some ways, it was the worst thing about the trip.

So it was a great relief for her when it was over and the back of the truck was opened to let her and the other cattle out. Their destination was a feedlot where the cattle were fattened up fast with a rich diet of food and chemicals. It looked a bit like the auction house they had just left, except this time the only animals to be seen were cattle—thousands and thousands of them in every direction. Also, the pens they were kept in were much bigger, allowing them some small space to move about. The feedlot itself was about as big as a football field divided into many such pens. But with so many animals crammed into each pen, their size made little difference.

Emily and Candy were herded into a pen not far from where the truck had parked. At first they were delighted to be in it just because they were out of the truck. Nothing could be worse than that, they thought. They hadn't been able to move in it, so it was wonderful to be able to stretch their legs again, even in a pen as small as this one.

"Oh, that feels good," Emily said holding her face up to the sun and stretching her back. "I thought I'd go crazy in there."

"Me, too," Candy said. "It felt like forever."

"You think that was bad?" a third heifer standing nearby said. She had been busy eating from a large, deep trough of feed, but when she heard Emily's voice, she walked over to where Emily was standing. "I was in one of those things for two days."

"Two days?" Emily and Candy exclaimed at once.

"Yes, two days," said the heifer.

"How did you survive?" Emily asked, amazed that someone could have withstood that kind of torture for two days.

"I don't know," the heifer said. "I was lucky I guess. Some of the cows I was traveling with didn't survive."

"What happened to them?" Emily wasn't sure she wanted to know, but a part of her had to find out.

"They couldn't take it," the heifer said. "It got so hot in there—the sun was beating down on us all day—and there was nothing to eat or drink, so they fell apart. Mind you, some of them were sick when they brought on board. Those ones died after only a few hours."

"Oh my," Emily said, and decided not to ask anymore. Sometimes that was best. She was just grateful that her own ride, bad as it was, had been brief. "This pen isn't very big," she finally said, changing the subject. "Not at all like the range I grew up on. That was huge. It went on forever. This is tiny."

"It sure is," Candy said. "And there are so many of us in here. How are we supposed to keep from bumping into one another?"

"You can't," the heifer who had traveled for two days said. "There's almost no room to move. But the food sure is good. Delicious. I eat it all day. So do most of the others. It's all there is to do."

The heifer was right, Emily learned. The food was terrific. It was grass mainly, but there was some grain in it as well. Emily loved it. That was a good thing because it wasn't all the heifer was right about—there really was nothing else to do.

"This is great," she said to Candy after a few mouthfuls. "In fact, I think it's the best food I've ever tasted."

"I think so, too," Candy replied after a big swallow. "I wonder what makes it taste so good."

"I don't really care," Emily said, "I'm just going to eat as much of it as I can."

So she did. First, she ate great heaps of the grass and grain mixture, but after a month or so, the amount of grass was reduced and the amount of grain increased. Soon it was nothing but grain, and she and Candy thought that was terrific.

So much eating and no exercise also made her bigger. If there hadn't been so many other animals to bump into, it would have taken her less than a minute to walk from one side of the pen to the other. On the range, she had been able to run alongside Jack without ever worrying about reaching the end. Here, the end was always in sight. So all she could do was eat and eat and eat and eat.

Other than the food, the only thing that changed was the weather. It got really cold suddenly and then it began to snow. It sure looked pretty coming down from the gray clouds, and Emily and Candy were glad to see it at first. At least it broke their routine, and they were sick of having nothing to do all day. Emily knew every square inch of the pen by heart, and none of it was much to look at. Before the snow, it was mostly mud. The snow covered the mud briefly in a broad blanket of white. But it was gone almost in no time. It didn't stand a chance, not with a hundred or more cows tramping through it and dropping their waste on it. But the snow left untouched on the pens beyond the fields was nice to look at, and sometimes Emily enjoyed watching birds leave delicate tracks in it when they touched down looking for food.

About a foot fell in two days, after which the skies cleared again as if somebody had wiped away the gray with a sponge. The sun came out, too, so Emily was able to enjoy its rays on her face and on her now very broad back for a short time each day. It was the only relief she got from the cold, which was severe. The onset of winter meant Emily's coat had grown heavy and shaggy, but still she was cold. She could see her breath hang in front of her face like a small, hesitant cloud. The water in the trough froze solid, and the man who put fresh food out for them had to come by all the time and break it up. There was no shelter, just a short overhang at one end of the pen, so when it got really cold, they had to huddle together for warmth, forming what looked like one enormous cow when they did.

Emily remembered the winter in the barn where she had been born. That seemed so long ago now. She had been safe there with Marigold, and thought the whole world was waiting beyond the window for her to enjoy. How wrong she had been. Except for those few months on the range with Jack and the others, life hadn't been much fun at all. She felt relatively safe in the feedlot, and Candy wasn't bad company, but Emily wasn't happy. Life was so boring, and despite all those promises she had made to herself about breaking free and being different from other cows, here she was with a hundred of them doing the same thing in the same place.

"Candy, do you think this will ever end?" she asked as she pressed herself against her friend for warmth and comfort.

"I don't know, but I sure wish it would. I liked the summer much better."

"Me, too," Emily said. "It's a good thing my coat has grown."

"No kidding," Candy said, "but even so."

It got even colder, and some of the cows in the other pens started getting sick. That was really bad because, with so many animals crowded together, if one got sick, the others might also get sick. A veterinarian visited all the time with bottles and needles and other medicines to make them better, but some died anyway. All Emily could do was feel sorry for them and look away.

No, it hadn't been much of a year, she thought. Not much of a life either. She often looked back on her days on the range and the time she spent playing with Jack and nuzzling close to her mother. What had happened to them? Where had they gone? What had become of Jack and Marigold? Part of her didn't like to imagine it. Had they been taken to an auction yard, too? Had they been crammed into a truck with no food or water or room to move? Did they have to be inside it for two days? And what about now? Were they in a pen like hers where there was nothing to do but eat?

What would happen next? That's what Emily thought about most. It was a funny question because it made her feel afraid and hopeful at the same time. Afraid, because of all the dreadful things that had happened to her so far, and hopeful because it was only through change that things would improve. Her little voice told her that, and she believed it. Maybe next time, it promised her, with a little more luck...

"What do you think?" she asked Candy one day after she'd been thinking hard about the future.

"What do I think about what?" Candy asked, looking up blankly from her food.

Emily paused before she replied. "Oh, never mind," she finally said, looking out at the fields beyond the fence. She decided maybe it was best not to let Candy in on her thoughts. She was always asking Candy to guess about the future, and like her, she never had any answers. What was the point? "I was just wondering," she said.

"Wondering what?" Candy asked, going back to her food.

"Wondering everything," Emily said. "About my mother and Jack and me and you."

"What about me and you?"

"I don't know, but I have a feeling we're not going to be here forever."

"No?" Candy asked nervously, looking up from the trough. "Where do you think we're going?"

"I don't know," Emily said, "but somewhere. Somewhere..."

"Somewhere better?" Candy asked.

"I don't know," Emily said. "But I sure wish I did."

Chapter Eight

A Deal's a Deal

When the time came, it didn't take Mr. Lansing long to decide to sell Emily at auction. She was too scrawny to keep.

"What do you think, Ted?" he asked his brother, just to see if he agreed. "See any point in keepin' her?"

Ted looked briefly at Emily and shook his head. "Nah. She's not getting' bigger fast enough. We could give her another few months on the range, but winter's comin' and that means spendin' money on hay. I say we lose her."

"I agree," said Mr. Lansing. "Not when we've had so many other good ones this year." Both he and Ted had been pleased with most of the calves born that year, and if beef prices stayed high, they expected to make a lot of money when it came time to sell them. Emily was an exception, but there were always exceptions. They knew that in ranching they had to take the good with the bad.

"Straight to the slaughterhouse?" Ted asked. "We might get a few bucks for her there."

"Nah, like I said, I think we'll try her at auction," Mr. Lansing said. "Let someone else decide what to do with her."

"Suits me," Ted said. He was pleased because it meant he was to have his day out at the auction yard after all. He could already taste the steak he was going to have afterward.

"The steer looks good, doesn't he?" Mr. Lansing asked, looking at Jack. Unlike Emily, he had put on a lot of weight during the summer. "We'll make a lot of money from him."

"Yeah, one of the best," Ted said.

"Strange how he and the heifer stick together, isn't it?" Mr. Lansing said. He hadn't given it much thought until then, but he couldn't help noticing it now.

"Huh?" Ted muttered. He hadn't noticed anything. "Oh, I guess so," he said for his brother's sake, and then forgot about it.

Later at the auction yard, Ted met up with his friends and made plans for the evening. Before selling Emily and the others, he decided to check out what else was for sale. Maybe there was something worth picking up if the price was right.

The pens were like a checkerboard, except each square was filled with animals. Ted and other buyers and sellers were allowed a bird's eye view of all the animals from an overhead ramp. It meant they didn't have to spend a lot of time moving from one pen to another. Some pens were under a roof, but most weren't, which meant that if it rained, they quickly became mud baths. The overhead ramp was good for keeping out of that, too. But today was warm and dry, so Ted was enjoying himself. Nothing much to look at though, he thought. The two old horses with swayed backs wouldn't fetch much. "Straight to the butcher with them," he said to himself.

The pig with her innards hanging out looked pretty rough. "Prolapsed uterus," Ted said to one of his buddies as they looked her up and down.

"Yeah," said his friend, "but it doesn't much matter when they turn her into bacon."

"True," Ted said, and walked on.

The goat caught his attention just because it was making so much noise. "Funny, what people try and sell, isn't it?" he said to his friend. "Maybe someone wants it for a pet."

"Or meat," his friend suggested.

"Yeah?" Ted had never heard of anyone eating goat.

"Sure," said his friend, "people'll eat anything."

"Some people," Ted said, and they both laughed.

Ted wandered into the auction barn because it was time for his animals to be sold, and he was hoping for a good price. Granted, they didn't have much going for them, he reminded himself, but you never know what people want or what they will pay. He and his friend sat near the front, close to the ring where the cattle would be brought out to be viewed. That way they could see the animals up close. It also helped the auctioneer, who relied on the slightest motion to tell him if someone was interested in buying. Sometimes the motion could be as subtle as a nod or a discreet wave of someone's hand. So he had to keep a sharp eye out all the time.

When the auctioneer described an animal, he spoke so fast that to people who didn't know what he was saying, it sounded like total nonsense.

"WhaddoIwhaddoIwhaddoIbidforthishereheifer400pounds?" he said when he asked what the bid was for a 400-pound heifer. But it made sense to the ranchers because they knew the code. They knew the auctioneer would post the animal's weight and expected price per pound in red lights. Then when the animal was sold, he would record the price it fetched as well.

As Ted expected, the two horses went really cheaply. He was surprised that anyone wanted them. The sick pigs didn't fetch much either, but there was a meat producer in the audience who figured he could use them. People laughed when the goat was brought in, but someone bought it. Ted never found out why. He wasn't disappointed with what he got for Emily and the others though. Jim Shank of Shank Beef Ltd. bought them and he said he might be able to make something of them.

"Even that one?" Ted said, pointing at Emily.

"Maybe," Jim said. "Maybe if she's fed right and enough, we can put a few pounds on her, and she'll be worth something then."

"All I can say is good luck," Ted said.

"Hey, that's the meat business, isn't it?" Jim said. "Nothing but luck."

"Yeah, and most of it's bad," Ted replied. Both of them laughed.

"So, goin' straight to the feedlot with 'em?" Ted continued.

"Yeah," Jim said, "I figure I'll leave 'em there a few months, fatten 'em up and then get 'em slaughtered."

"It's a risk," Ted said. "You might not get back what you pay the feedlot to fill 'em."

"I know," Jim said, "that's where the luck comes in." They both laughed again. "But I still say it's worth a try."

"And people sure like the grain-fed stuff, don't they?" Ted said.

"Oh yeah. Customers eat it up, so to speak. Makes the beef real juicy. But hey, Ted, I don't have to tell you that."

"No," said Ted, laughing and patting his stomach, which was a little bigger than it had been a year ago. "You sure don't."

When Mr. Shank delivered Emily and the rest of his newly bought cattle to Enderby's feedlot, he greeted Ed Enderby like an old friend. They had done business together for years and knew each other well. But it was still business, so Mr. Shank wanted to be sure he would be getting his money's worth from Mr. Enderby.

"I'd like to get a good price for 'em at slaughter, Ed," he said to Mr. Enderby as the truck was unloaded and Candy and Emily were herded out.

"Don't worry, Jim, I'll do my best. I always do, you know that. It'll be four months of the best grain money can buy. And the chemicals help, too. You know I gotta pump 'em full of antibiotics to keep 'em from getting sick."

"Makes 'em grow faster, too," Jim said.

"Yeah, it does. I go through tons of 'em every year. But you gotta admit, Jim, you're not givin' me much to work with. Look at that one over there," he said nodding at Emily.

"Yeah, she's the worst of the bunch," Jim said, "but I got faith, even in her."

"Okay," Mr. Enderby said as the cows were herded into the nearest pen. "It's your money. But you know I can't make promises."

"I know," Jim said. "So how many head you got right now?"

"About ten thousand," Mr. Enderby replied.

"Hey, you're gettin' busier," Jim said.

"Yeah, but not busy enough. Henderson's over in the next county has fifty thousand."

"Don't worry, you'll get there soon, Ed," Jim said, slapping Ed's back. "Now I gotta go."

"Okay, see yah soon," Ed replied as Jim climbed into his pickup. "Come by whenever you wanna check up on 'em."

"Why? Can't I trust you?" Jim said, kind of laughing and kind of not.

"'Course you can," Ed said, not sure how serious Jim was being. "I just mean…"

"I know what you mean," Jim said, driving away. "See ya soon."

Months later, after the worst of the snow was gone, Jim was pleased with what he saw. Even Emily was significantly bigger. She still wasn't as big as the others, but a good size nonetheless. It would have taken well over two years to reach the size she was now if it weren't for Ed Enderby's intensive feeding and chemicals. This way he could get her to the slaughterhouse and make his money much faster.

"Great job," he said to Ed as they settled his bill. "I'll make a few bucks out of 'em yet."

"Yeah, I was kinda surprised myself," Ed said. "They turned out real well."

"Heard you lost some though."

"Yeah, a few got sick. It happens."

"Yeah, it does. That's why I'm gonna get these to slaughter before it happens to me."

"Right," Ed said. "Good luck."

It took about an hour for the calves, including Emily, to be herded onto Jim's truck.

"Okay, I'll be on my way," Jim said calling out the window of his cab. "Thanks again, Ed."

"No problem. Any time."

He watched as the truck started to pull away.

"Hey Jim," he called when the truck was almost out of his yard. "Something wrong with the back wheels?" They were wobbling, and Mr. Enderby didn't think Jim had noticed.

"What?" Jim called.

"I said, something wrong with those wheels?" Ed yelled again. By then Jim couldn't hear him. The truck's engine was making too much noise. So he waved him good-bye instead. Inside the trailer, the cattle were kicking and bellowing to get out, making it rock back and forth wildly on its springs.

Chapter Nine

The Rescue Ranch

*C*hris *didn't like Mr. Bridges.* He thought he was a jerk, and he was sure he didn't like kids. He didn't even say hello when Gina and Chris arrived at his ranch. "Who's that?" he growled when they appeared at his gate.

His gruffness riled Chris, who was all set to leave right away, but Gina didn't even notice it. Either she was weirder than Chris thought or she was used to it. She just sailed through the gate and threw herself at all the dogs that rushed up to greet them.

That was another thing. Chris had never seen so many dogs in one place before, and it made him nervous. There were big dogs, little dogs, long-haired dogs, short-haired dogs, black dogs, brown dogs, black-and-brown dogs, white-and-brown dogs, and white-and-black dogs. There were dogs with only one ear, with three legs, or no tail. Whatever the color or condition, there was a dog to fit the bill. All them barked at once as they crowded against each other to jump up on Chris and Gina. There were so many of them and they made so much noise that even Chris, who liked dogs—or so he thought—couldn't help being scared. When Mr. Bridges yelled at the dogs to "Keep quiet!" in a voice loud enough to wake Chris's dead grandmother in a cemetery all the way back in the city, Chris knew that being at the Rescue Ranch was a mistake he never wanted to make again. He just wanted to leave and never come back.

He would have right then if he hadn't noticed how unruffled Gina was. She wasn't just calm, she was enjoying herself. She knew all the dogs' names and treated each one like an old friend. "Hello, hello, hello," she sang lovingly as she reached over to pet one dog, then another, then another. There was always one more smiling face jumping up to lick hers, and she made time for all of them. "How are you, Bowser?" she said to the dog with one ear. "And you, Rufus?" to the dog with no tail. Rufus was so pleased that if he'd had a tail he would have thumped it back and forth like a drumstick. "And how's Bonnie?" she cooed, picking up a little brown mop of a dog. She held it under her arm knowing that Bonnie demanded nothing less. "Bonnie insists on her cuddles," Gina said to Chris as she scratched Bonnie under the chin. "Don't you sweetheart?"

She was so preoccupied in saying hello to the animals that she almost forgot to answer Mr. Bridges when he asked her who Chris was. In fact, he had to ask her twice. "Oh, sorry," she finally said, bending over to pet yet more dogs. "This is Chris. I met him yesterday at the rodeo. He said he wanted to meet you. Chris, this is Mr. Bridges."

"Hello," said Chris, extending his hand to shake Mr. Bridges's, the way he had been taught to do by his father. But Mr. Bridges didn't respond. He just stood there with his hands on his hips and stared.

"You like rodeos, kid?" he asked Chris with a voice that could grind rocks. Chris put down his hand.

"Um, not really," he said, deciding that if Gina and Mr. Bridges thought rodeos were cruel, he'd better think so, too. He didn't want to disagree with a man who looked as if he'd feel comfortable wrestling giants. Mr. Bridges was tall like Andrew, but while Andrew was thin like a giraffe, Mr. Bridges was like a grizzly bear with broad shoulders, a thick neck, and arms like clubs.

"Then what were you doing there?" Mr. Bridges asked, still growling.

"My stepdad took me and my mom," Chris said, more nervous than ever. Mr. Bridges was one of the most frightening people he'd ever met.

"His stepdad's the doctor," Gina said, her eyes still on the dogs, and Bonnie in particular.

"Ah yes," Mr. Bridges said. "I know him. He's a good man even if he does take you to rodeos."

Chris didn't know what to say.

"So do you like dogs, Chris?" Mr. Bridges asked in a way that sounded more like a threat than a question.

"Um, yes," Chris replied, because he did. At least he was sure of that. He just didn't like being around so many of them all at once. He was used to seeing one dog at a time, not thirty or forty.

"That's good," Mr. Bridges said. "I like a kid who likes dogs. Too many don't."

"Chris couldn't think of any kid who didn't like dogs, but he wasn't about to contradict an ogre like Mr. Bridges. Instead, he asked "How many have you got?" because he wanted to know and he figured it was a question Mr. Bridges might like to answer.

He was right. "Thirty-six," Mr. Bridges said, his eyes lighting up like candles. He was in his fifties, with the beginnings of white hair and a face that had been out in the sun too long, just like Mr. Lansing's. When Chris first saw him, he had looked kind of gray all over as well, as if he were only half-alive. But when he began talking about his dogs, the grayness disappeared. "And every one of 'em has his own story to tell," Mr. Bridges added, as proud as if he were talking about his own children.

"Really?" Chris asked, not sure if Mr. Bridges was suggesting that the dogs could talk. He seemed like such a nutcase that Chris wouldn't have put it past him.

"Really," Mr. Bridges replied, kneeling down to put his arm around a big, shaggy brown dog that sat beside him. He was smiling a wide grin now and the grayness had vanished completely. What's more, he didn't look as frightening as he had when Chris was introduced. The dogs weren't making as much noise either. "This one here, Lara, I got from a trash can when she was a pup. Someone had just tossed her in it. Isn't that right, Lara?" he said, stroking Lara's ears. Clearly Lara loved it and adored Mr. Bridges.

"Really?" Chris asked. "Why would someone do that?"

"You tell me," Mr. Bridges said, his anger returning. "Why do people do the things they do? Do you know?"

"Ummm," Chris began, wondering if he was supposed to answer. He had no idea why people did the things they did.

"Lara would have died if I hadn't rescued her," Mr. Bridges said, tenderly now because he was talking about Lara. "So would half the dogs here. No, not half the dogs, *all* the dogs. They all would have been dead if I hadn't rescued them."

"Wow," Chris said. He was impressed. Now that the dogs weren't jumping or barking so much, he was able to get a better look at them, and they did look pretty nice. Even the ones with a missing ear or tail looked happy. They were all well fed and had shiny coats, and none of them cowered or hid the way abused dogs sometimes do.

"Mr. Bridges likes dogs better than people," Gina said. "And horses and cows, too. Isn't that right, Mr. Bridges?"

"You think that's strange, Chris?" Mr. Bridges growled again. He eyed Chris carefully.

"Ummm," Chris mumbled, because once again he didn't know what to say. Sure he liked dogs, but better than people? Better than his mom or dad or Andrew or the friends he'd left behind in the city? He didn't think so.

"A lot of people think it's strange," Mr. Bridges continued. He and Gina started to walk toward his house, so Chris decided he had better follow. Some of the dogs ran off to play. None of them lived in cages so they were free to run around as much as they liked.

Others followed Mr. Bridges and Gina. "I've been around a lot of people and a lot of animals in my life, and I gotta say I prefer the animals. Isn't that right, Chester?" he asked, bending down to stroke a black spaniel-like dog with long floppy ears that dragged in the dirt. "That's why I bought this ranch, to look after 'em. What do you think of it?"

When Chris and Gina had ridden toward it on their bicycles, Chris couldn't help noticing how grand it looked. Unlike the rest of the country around the town, the Rescue Ranch had lots of trees on it so that you knew you were approaching it from a long way off. It was like a small green city in the middle of a plain of dust. Then as they rode closer, Chris noticed that there were cows by the trees. The trees were so leafy that it was hard to see the cows through them, but they were there, huddled under the branches for shade. That surprised him because all the other cows he'd seen had been out in the sunshine. He didn't think cows liked shade.

There was also a small red house on the ranch where Mr. Bridges lived, a barn near the house where Mr. Bridges kept his supplies and feed for the animals, a couple of white pickup trucks with "Rescue Ranch" printed in red letters on the doors, and a sign that read "Beware of dogs," on the gate by the road. "Gina," Chris said nervously as they rode past the sign. "Did you see that?"

"Yeah," Gina said without much concern. "It doesn't mean anything. All Mr. Bridges's dogs are friendly."

Now that Chris had been at the ranch a while, he realized she was right. All the dogs *were* friendly, and the longer Chris was around them, the friendlier they became. The got quieter, too. At one point, they stopped barking altogether.

"Don't look so surprised," Mr. Bridges said when it happened. He even managed to laugh for the first time since Chris arrived. "This is the way it is around here most of the time. People don't realize it because they only come for a few minutes, and the dogs always go crazy when they see a new face. But once they get used to you, they accept you and they stop barking. It's just that most people are scared off by the noise they make at first, so most people never get to find out how nice they are."

"Well, they sure are nice now," Chris said, stroking a big, black German shepherd–like dog named Brutus.

"Glad you think so, Chris," said Mr. Bridges, who didn't look or sound nearly as ferocious as he had before. "Would you like to see the rest of the ranch?"

"Okay," said Chris, who was beginning to feel much less uncomfortable.

"Then Gina and I will show you."

It wasn't large as ranches go, no more than 150 acres, about the size of a small village. The biggest commercial ranches were hundreds of square miles in size. They had to be big to graze so many thousands of animals. But the Rescue Ranch wasn't that kind of place, Mr. Bridges explained. He had only thirty-two cattle, and he didn't raise them for beef. His ranch was there so the animals on it could live out their lives in peace and comfort. No one was going to hurt or frighten them, he said, and they could do whatever they liked as long as they stayed within its boundaries and didn't hurt each other.

"How do you get them?" Chris asked walking out toward the pasture where the cattle were grazing.

"In different ways," Mr. Bridges said. "Sometimes I buy them at cattle auctions and sometimes I get them directly from a rancher. One of them is a 4-H cow that a boy couldn't bear to sell for slaughter when his project was done."

"But how do you know which ones to choose?" Chris asked. "There are so many. I see them everywhere."

"Call it a sixth sense," Mr. Bridges said. "Or maybe just a whim. All I know is that sometimes I'll hear about a particular cow that a rancher doesn't want—maybe it's too big or too small, or maybe it causes too much trouble. And then I'll buy it so it can live here."

"So what do cows like to do?" Chris asked. It seemed to him as if they didn't like to do much of anything.

Mr. Bridges laughed a second time. Then he explained that while the dogs liked to play and sleep, and the horses ran around and grazed, cows were placid animals that were happy just knowing that one day was going to be pretty much like the one before.

Chris didn't understand that.

"I'll show you," Mr. Bridges replied, leading him and Gina to where the cows had wandered off. "You see," he said, gesturing with an open hand to where the cows were grazing and resting under the trees. "They like to do that. And unlike the cattle you see on commercial farms, my cattle are never afraid. You can drive right up to them in a pickup truck and they won't get nervous because they know no one's going to hurt them. Drive up to a cow or a steer on a commercial ranch and they'll probably run for their lives. Here they stay still."

"Oh," Chris said, "so I guess they're not too much fun to have around."

"Well, that depends on what you call fun," Mr. Bridges said, smiling again. "Cows are a lot smarter than most people think they are."

"That's what Gina tells me," Chris said.

"Well, Gina's a smart girl," Mr. Bridges said. But Gina wasn't around to hear. She had gone off to join a couple of cows under the trees. "For example, do you think a cow or a steer can recognize his own name?"

"I don't know," said Chris. "I never thought about it."

"Then watch this." Mr. Bridges called out in a loud voice: "Orion! Come here, Orion. Come to Daddy."

Daddy? Chris thought, wincing. It made him a little sick to think of a grown man as big as Mr. Bridges calling himself daddy to a cow. But he was still nervous around Mr. Bridges, and knew better than to say anything about it. But what do you know? When he did, Orion, a shining black steer as big as a minivan, shuffled over to where he stood.

Cattle don't have expressive faces like dogs, so it was hard for

Chris to tell if Orion was pleased to see Mr. Bridges. But he did stand patiently while Mr. Bridges stroked his face and told him what a beautiful boy he was.

"So what do you think, Chris?" Mr. Bridges asked, inviting Chris to stroke Orion.

"I think he's cool," Chris said, reaching up to pat Orion on the nose. "He's not going to charge me, is he?" he asked, stepping back nervously.

"No, no, don't worry about that," Mr. Bridges said. "As long as you're calm around him, he'll be calm around you. But you do have to be careful around animals as big as these. You don't want to get in the way of one when they're running."

"No," said Chris, who was still a bit wary, despite Mr. Bridges's assurance. Orion was huge—it would have taken thirty boys Chris's size to equal him—and Chris didn't want to do anything to upset him.

"Hey, Chris," Gina called, "come and meet Cumin."

"What?" called Chris, who was preoccupied with keeping out of Orion's way.

"I said, come and meet Cumin," Gina called again. "She's my favorite."

"Go on," Mr. Bridges said to Chris, "but be careful."

"I will," Chris said, giving Orion an extra wide berth as he walked slowly to where Gina was standing with a sandy-colored cow under the trees.

"This is Cumin," she said, stroking the cow along her face. "Isn't she beautiful? She's my favorite of all Mr. Bridges's cows. Don't tell the others I said that."

Chris laughed a little nervously. It was strange the way Gina and Mr. Bridges seemed to believe that the animals could speak and think almost as if they were human. He knew dogs could think—sort of—but he didn't think cows could, at least not in the same way.

"So what do you think?" Gina asked, flicking her bright red hair off her face. A breeze had come up making her hair blow all over the place so that her head looked as if it were on fire.

"I think she's nice," Chris said as he stroked Cumin.

"No, I don't mean Cumin, although I'm glad you like her. I mean what do you think of the whole ranch?"

"I like it…I guess," Chris said. He was still a bit unsure of Mr. Bridges, but judging from the way Mr. Bridges spoke to his animals, he wasn't quite the monster Chris thought he was when they met. And Chris did like the dogs. They were fun now that he knew not to be afraid of them. The horses were beautiful, too, especially a gray one that tossed its mane around as if it were showing off like a model in a show. But the cows? If he were going to be honest, he'd have to say that it was hard to get excited about them, no matter what Gina and Mr. Bridges said. They were okay, but kind of boring, too. He knew better than to say so, however.

"So do you think you'd like to come back?" Gina asked. "Like I said, I come every weekend to give Mr. Bridges some time away. He likes to visit his brother in town so they can play cards. I help feed the dogs and groom the horses, and in winter when the horses and cows can't graze, I help feed them."

"It sounds like a lot of work," Chris said. All the feeding and grooming, and then more feeding in winter.

"It is, but I like it," Gina said. "I like being around the animals."

"I guess," Chris said.

"So what about you? Do you want to come again?"

"I dunno," Chris said, shrugging his shoulders. "I'll see."

He did go back, though. Not as often as Gina wanted him to, but until school started and when he wasn't visiting his dad in the city, it gave him something to do when the days stretched long and lonely in front of him. Even after school began, he carried on visiting because by then he'd grown fond of Mr. Bridges's dogs, and his mom and Andrew still hadn't kept their promise to get him one of his own.

Starting school had been a struggle. The first few days were as bad as he imagined they would be because, apart from Gina, everyone and everything was new, and Chris was a stranger everywhere he went. A few kids would greet him, but mostly he kept to himself.

"So how was it, Chris?" his mom asked after his first day.

"I hate it! I wish I'd never come to the country! I wish I was back at my old school with my old friends! I hate it here! Hate it, hate it, hate it!"

Helene said she understood, and promised that things would improve if only Chris would let them. All it would take was time. Chris sulked and mumbled, "What does she know?" up the stairs to his room where he shut the door and flung himself face first onto his bed. There was no way things would ever change, he thought. He would have to stay in his room forever.

But gradually, he decided his mother might be right. His first week at school was miserable, but the second, he had to admit, was a little better. The third week was even better than that. Luckily for Chris, he was a good athlete and that made a big difference. When the other boys saw him in phys. ed. class, they were eager to make friends with him. They even suggested he try out for the school football team. That pleased him a lot, and he said he would. It made him believe that he just might learn to cope with all these strange surrounding after all.

There was a problem with Gina, however. All the other kids thought she was a freak, and compared to them, she was. She certainly looked different with her brightly colored hair, her outrageous makeup, and her wild clothes. The things she said often made her stand out, too. Most of the kids in the school came from ranching families, or families that sold equipment, supplies, or services to ranchers, so they thought she was odd for not eating meat. And when she talked about moving to the city to become an actress or a model, they made fun of her for dreaming. They had to admit, though, that she was pretty enough to be a model. She would be the prettiest girl in the school if only she wiped off some of that ugly makeup.

Even so, Chris liked her. In fact, it was because she was so different that he found her interesting. No matter how nice the other kids were when they saw how fast he was on the football field, Chris had to admit that deep down he was different from them, too. Gina was more like a city kid than his other schoolmates. She wouldn't have had any trouble fitting in at his old school—at least she would have a lot less trouble than she was having now. The way she dressed wouldn't have seemed so strange, and the kids might even have accepted the things she said. It was only out here in the middle of nowhere that they branded her in the same way that Emily's *L* branded her.

Not only that, Gina was smart. She always put her hand up first when their teacher, Miss Dressler, asked a question, and she usually had the right answer. Eventually Miss Dressler stopped letting her answer just to give the other kids a chance. But Gina wasn't a show-off about it. She didn't boast that she was more clever than everyone else; she just was. Chris liked talking to her, and he went with her to the Rescue Ranch whenever he didn't have a football game, wasn't playing video games with the guys at the only arcade in town, or visiting his dad in the city.

But it caused him problems. "Why do you hang out with weird Gina?" the guys asked him when they were at the arcade or skateboarding.

"I dunno," Chris said. He didn't want to come out and admit he liked her because they might tease him if he did. But he didn't want to agree with them either because that would be lying. All he did was say, "She's okay."

"No, she's not," said Lenny, a guy Chris didn't like much, but hung around with anyway because he was on the football team. "She's weird. She looks weird, and she says weird stuff. Like yesterday when she said that the makeup she wears isn't tested on animals. What does that mean? Like, whoever heard of animals wearing makeup?" Lenny joked to the others in the group.

They obliged him by laughing because Lenny wasn't just on the football team, he was also its best player.

What Gina had tried to explain was that most makeup was tested on animals in laboratories before it's sold to women in stores, and that animals suffered and died because of it. But some companies, she said, made what they call "cruelty-free" products that aren't tested on animals, so those were the only products that she and her mother bought. Chris thought it made sense if it was true about the laboratories. So did Miss Dressler and a few of the girls in the class. But Lenny and his group just laughed.

"Doesn't that bother you?" Chris asked Gina when they were walking home from school one day.

"No," Gina said, but Chris didn't believe her. It would have bothered him if the other kids had laughed at him, so he knew it had to hurt Gina, too.

"Really?" he asked. "Not at all?"

"Maybe a bit," Gina confessed. "But it's like Mr. Bridges says, I think animals are nicer than people so I prefer to be with them."

"But doesn't that get kind of lonely?" Chris asked. "I mean, I like the animals at Mr. Bridges's ranch, too, but I think I'd miss it if you weren't there 'cause the animals can't talk back to me."

"They can if you listen," Gina said. Gina believed that animals had their own special way of communicating, and if people opened themselves up to understanding what an animal meant when it rubbed itself against something, or ran around in a circle, or barked or mooed in a certain way, then people would be able to figure out what the animal was trying to say. When she explained this, Chris thought it was strange at first, but the more he went to the ranch, the more he understood what she meant. It was plain to him when the dogs wanted something and when they were excited and when they were angry. He knew when they were jealous of another dog, and most important, he knew when they liked someone. Even so, he knew he'd miss it if he didn't have people to talk to as well. Maybe not people like Lenny, but other people like his family and his real friends. No matter what Gina and Mr. Bridges said, he believed they thought the same thing. After all, they liked talking to each other and to him, so the animals couldn't be enough.

"I don't understand why Gina doesn't make it easier for herself," Chris said to his mother one afternoon when he got home from school.

"What do you mean?" Helene asked. She was clearing up the kitchen after having Sylvia Lansing to lunch. She saw Mrs. Lansing a lot now, and Chris hadn't heard her complain about being bored in a while. "Sylvia," his mom had said, "is one of the most unusual people I've ever met. She's always surprising me." Helene wasn't nearly as unhappy as she was when they went to the rodeo, and now it looked as if she might get a part-time job at the local library.

"I mean, if she didn't wear that funny makeup and color her hair that way, the other kids in school wouldn't think she was strange," Chris said, putting his schoolbooks on the table.

"Perhaps she likes wearing makeup and coloring her hair," Helene said. "I agree, it is odd that someone her age does it so much, but if her mom doesn't mind, why should you?"

"It's not that I mind; it's that other kids do," Chris said. Why couldn't parents understand things the first time? It was so frustrating having to explain things again and again. "They think she's weird because of everything she does, and I think she's weird for not trying to be like everyone else."

"Well, the world would be a pretty dull place if everyone were like everyone else," Chris's mom said. "That's why I like Sylvia so much. She's one of the most unusual people I've ever met."

There she goes again, Chris thought. Parents could be so dense sometimes. "I guess so," he said. But then he couldn't let it go and added: "Like today, she said she likes animals better than people, and she likes spending time with animals better than she likes spending time with people. You know, the same kind of weird stuff Mr. Bridges says. Well, I don't think she should say things like that 'cause people will think she's different and won't want to know her, the way they don't want to know Mr. Bridges."

Coming home from the Rescue Ranch one day, Chris had asked Andrew all about Mr. Bridges and what the other people in the town thought of him. Andrew explained that ever since Mr. Bridges's wife had died in a car accident years ago, he had kept pretty much to himself apart from one brother who ran the local movie house. People liked him, Andrew said, but they couldn't understand what he was trying to do on his ranch.

"He's trying to be nice to his animals," Chris had said.

"I know," Andrew replied. "But people here have a different idea about animals. They make their living from raising them as beef, so they don't understand someone who just keeps them for the sake of keeping them."

"Do you understand it?" Chris asked.

Andrew waited a while before he answered. "To tell you the truth, Chris, not always. I do understand rescuing dogs because dogs are pets and people like having them around. Having horses makes some sense, too, because you can ride horses. But cattle? What are cattle good for except giving us meat and leather?"

"Mr. Bridges says they're good for themselves, and that's enough."

"Well, maybe, but not many people around here would agree."

"So don't people around here like Mr. Bridges?" Chris asked. "He is kinda scary at first, but not when you get to know him. Then he isn't scary at all."

Andrew laughed and said no one found him scary, although he agreed that Mr. Bridges might seem that way at first. "No, it's just that given the way Mr. Bridges thinks and the kind of life he leads, they don't warm to him the way they might if he were different. Do you understand?"

"Not really," Chris said. "You mean they don't talk to him?"

"No, no," Andrew said. "Everyone talks to him whenever he comes into town to buy something or go to the post office or see me. It's only that people think he's a man who prefers to be by himself or at least with his animals. So they find him a little odd."

"Well, I like him," Chris said. "I didn't at first, but I do now. And I like his animals, too."

"Sure you do," Andrew said, "and there's no reason why you shouldn't."

Later that evening after Chris went to bed, Andrew asked Helene if she thought it was wise to let Chris spend so much time at the Rescue Ranch. "Do you think he's getting some funny ideas?" he asked.

"What kind of funny ideas?" Helene asked. She was busy trying to learn some calligraphy strokes that Mrs. Lansing had shown her that afternoon.

"He said something about how we shouldn't put any worth on cows or dogs because they're already worth something to themselves."

"That doesn't sound so bad to me," Helene said. "In fact, it sounds kind of nice."

"Maybe," Andrew said, "but around here people might find that kind of talk unusual, and I don't want Chris to be made to feel left out, the way Gina is."

"I like Gina," Helene said. "Don't you?"

"Of course I do," Andrew said. "I think she's a sweet kid, never mind all that makeup and dyed hair. But she isn't like the other kids around here and she suffers for it. I know she does because her mother mentions it sometimes when she comes to see me at the office."

"That is hard," Helene agreed, "but I admire her for being herself and not giving in to what other people think she should be, and I'd like to think I'm raising Chris to be the same."

"To be thought of as weird by the other kids?"

"Andrew!" Helene shouted. "Just what century do you think this is?"

"Sorry," he said. Nevertheless he kept on worrying about Chris, just as Chris kept worrying about Gina, who kept on doing all the things that made Chris worry about her in the first place. And as summer blended into fall, and fall into winter, and winter into a brand new year, Chris remained as confused as ever.

He stayed friends with Gina, no matter what Lenny and the other guys said, and he kept going to the Rescue Ranch to see the animals and Mr. Bridges. It took time, but eventually he came to understand a little better why she liked coming to the ranch and why she said the things she did about the animals on it. He had to agree that the more he got to know the animals, the more he got to like them. The dogs were still his favorites, but even the cows were starting to grow on him. He wasn't going to admit that to anyone except Gina and Mr. Bridges—and even then he was a little embarrassed—but they were. He liked their gentleness and the way their eyes looked as big as marbles.

Yet at the same time he understood why Andrew said that most people who lived in the area made their money from cattle, and had for the past hundred years. In some ways, things had been so much simpler in the city, he thought. Out here Chris was being pulled in two directions like a wishbone—Gina, Mr. Bridges, and the animals on one side, and almost his whole school and the rest of the town on the other—and he didn't know what to do about it. And sometimes just like a wishbone, he thought he would snap from it. He tried not to think about it, but then something would happen—Gina would get teased or Mr. Bridges would say something nasty about someone Chris liked—and it would flare up all over again. Lying in his bed at night staring at the ceiling, he wished something would happen to make everything clear.

The last time he felt so confused was when his parents divorced. His mother had said that no one was right and no one was wrong; she and his dad simply couldn't live together anymore. He couldn't believe that. If no one was wrong, then no one should be mad, he thought. So it only made sense that they stay married.

"If only things were that easy," Helene had said.

"Well, why can't they be?" Chris shouted. "They could be if you tried."

"We have tried, Chris, but it's not enough," Helene explained. "You'll see for yourself one day. It's not fair, but life is more complicated than that. I wish it weren't, but it is."

Well, he was seeing for himself. Life was more complicated than he wanted it to be, and it wasn't fair. He didn't like it one bit.

Chapter Ten

On the Run

"*Oh no,*" *Emily said,* looking at Mr. Shank's enormous box trailer as it pulled into the feedlot driveway. "Not this. Not again."

By now she was smart enough to know it didn't pay to disobey the cowboys since they always got their way in the end, but the box was different. She hated the box more than anything, and she didn't think she could bear to ride in it a third time. So when the ramp dropped and Emily stared into the trailer's dark, dirty, smelly prison again, she went a little crazy. She remembered what the cow next to her on her first day in the feedlot had said about having to travel for two days without food or water, and she knew she couldn't stand that. She didn't know how long she would have to travel this time—two hours or two days—but even two minutes in the box was something she wasn't prepared to endure. So she had to fight, just as the cattle at the auction yard had all those months ago. When it was time to get on the trailer, Emily refused to budge.

"What are you doing?" Candy asked when she saw Emily stand her ground. "You know you can't win. None of us can."

"Who says I can't?" Emily mooed, her hooves dug firmly into the ground as the cowboys whacked her with their sticks. The sticks hurt, but inside the box was worse. Nothing was worse than that.

"Emily!" Candy called. "Don't be so stubborn. It'll be okay."

"How do you know?" Emily grunted, still refusing to move. The cowboys were really angry now and were starting to put their boots to her.

"Emily!" Candy called again.

The cowboys were determined and Emily wasn't used to standing up to them. Their blows and kicks hurt her again and again, but the little voice inside her kept urging her not to give in. It reminded her that she was special, and that she didn't have to be like all the other cows if she didn't want to be. And now was the time to prove it.

"I will," Emily said to herself, "I will."

What she didn't anticipate was the cowboys using other cattle to push her. It was one of their favorite strategies. They would round up a group of animals behind a particularly difficult one, and then force that animal to move with the stream. There was no way Emily could resist it. The pressure was too great.

"What are you doing?" Emily called to the animals behind her. "You don't want to go into that awful thing, do you?" They didn't, but the cowboys knew how to handle them, and after only a little more struggle, all of them, including Emily, were shut tight inside the trailer again.

It was just as bad as before—filthy, dark, noisy, and packed so tight that Emily couldn't take one step forward or one step back. All she could do was kick against the wall she was pressed against. It was a strong steel panel designed to withstand a lot of weight. "I want out, I want out," she moaned as the truck engine started to rumble and its wheels started to turn. "I want out of here!"

Other cows were moaning and kicking, too, causing the trailer to rock on its springs almost like a ship at sea. It made a terrible racket.

"Why bother?" asked Candy, as Emily continued to kick. "You know you're trapped. Save your strength."

"Save it for what?" Emily asked, still angry and still kicking. "Save my strength for what? We don't know what they're going to do to us next."

"I know," Candy said, "but we still can't get out of here unless they let us out."

Emily, however, wasn't so sure. She was right in the middle of the trailer where there was a small door built into the panel. It was supposed to be fastened shut with bolts, but there was a crack where it should have closed. The crack allowed a sliver of daylight to get through, and that gave Emily all the hope she needed. Emily kicked hard on the door, so that it rattled. Because of the sliver of light, she sensed that if she kicked it hard enough, it might give way. At least it was worth a try.

It also wasn't the only thing that was different about this truck. The other two trucks Emily had ridden in were steadier than this one. They swayed slightly when they went around corners, and that always made her and the other cattle nervous. But when the road straightened out, the ride was always fairly smooth. Not this time. This truck wobbled. None of the cattle could get a sure footing because the trailer lurched even when it was going straight.

"I don't like this," Candy said, trying for what seemed like the hundredth time to stand still and straight. "I'm going to fall."

Emily thought she would fall, too. She had been so busy kicking the door that she hadn't noticed the truck's roll, but now that the other animals on board had calmed down and stopped their kicking, she felt it clearly. It made her kick even harder.

"Emily!" Candy called again. "Em ..."

But she couldn't finish because at that moment the trailer went around a sharp bend and lurched violently. It sounded as if all its screws and bolts were straining just to hold it together.

"Candy," Emily said nervously. "Caaaa..." But she couldn't

finish either because suddenly there was a terrible BAM! and the truck stopped abruptly.

"Whooooooah," the cattle aboard moaned. "Ohhhhhhh, what's happened?"

It was chaos inside. It had been hard enough keeping their footing before, but the truck stopped so suddenly that cattle started falling on top of each other. Some hurt themselves badly. "Ohhhhh," they moaned. "Help! Help!"

Emily was in a panic. She managed to keep from falling, but she was almost frozen with fear. She didn't know what to do or where to turn. It was as if the whole world had crashed around her. She stayed that way for several minutes until slowly she began to breathe again and collect her wits. "Oh no," she said, looking around her at the crush of animals thrown here and there against each other and against the sides of the truck. "What now?"

Then she smelled something. Something enticing, in fact, like perfume only better. It was fresh air, and it was blowing gently against her face. The side door she had been kicking against had broken open in the crash, and right there in front of her and all the others was a way out.

"Candy!" she cried with such excitement that she could barely get the words out. "Candy, look!"

Candy was frozen by fear, and didn't listen at first.

"Candy!" Emily mooed a third time. "We can get out. Look here. We can get out here."

It was a tight squeeze because the doorway was smaller than the one in the back of the trailer. But Emily was determined. Narrow or not, she was going to make it. This, she realized, was her chance.

"Candy" she called as she wedged herself through the passageway. "Come on! Follow me!"

"What?" Candy said, still disoriented. "Emily?"

"Come on, follow me," Emily repeated as she stepped onto the roadway looking around in every direction. Once again she felt free, the way she had on the range with Marigold and Jack before the cowboys had come to take away her freedom. "Candy, come on," she urged. "I'm leaving!"

"What do you mean, you're leaving?" Candy asked. "Leaving where?"

"I'm going away," Emily answered. "Away from here." The little voice inside her was screaming, "Go, go, go!"

"But you can't," Candy said. "What will happen to you?"

"I don't know," Emily said, "but I'm not waiting around here for more men to give more orders. Not anymore."

Just then, the men who had been driving the truck stepped out of the cab. They were shaken up, and they were panicking and yelling when they stepped onto the road. At first they didn't notice Emily, but she saw them and she knew she had to act fast.

"Candy," she said quickly, getting ready to charge. "It's now or never. Are you coming or aren't you?"

"Don't!" Candy mooed. "Don't! You'll get into trouble. Emily, come back!"

Trouble was nothing new to Emily. Apart from her first few weeks on the range, all she'd ever known was trouble, so she was ready to face it again now. The difference was that this time it would be trouble of her own making. "Good-bye, Candy," she called as she started to run. "Goody-bye!"

"Emily!" Candy called again.

But Emily didn't hear her. She was running too hard and too fast down the road. The truck drivers ran after her, yelling at the tops of their lungs, but they couldn't catch her. She was too fast and there were no fences or other cattle to hold her in this time. She was three times the size she had been when she was a young calf on the range, and after standing around the feedlot and eating for so long, her legs were stiff and sore. Running was no longer easy. She felt unsteady and thought a few times that she might fall. But the little voice kept urging her on. "Run," it said. "Run, run, run."

At that moment she realized what the voice had meant all along when it told her that she didn't have to be the same as other cattle.

She felt sorry for Candy and the other animals left behind in the trailer, and she worried for their safety. She worried for hers, too, but she couldn't go back and join them, not when she was finally free, not when there was nothing but the open road in front of her.

But the open road posed dangers of its own. Cars kept honking at her when they passed. Some of them even stopped so the people inside could get out and chase her. They couldn't catch her, but she was still afraid because people had been responsible for all her suffering, and she knew if she was going to survive this time, it would only be without people. It meant that she would never trust a person again. It was hard keeping out of their way though. They turned up wherever she went, calling and chasing after her. Some of them had guns, which they fired into the air. She kept running along the main road, looking for a way off of it, but there were fences on either side of it, and it was only when a small side road finally opened up that she was able to make her escape.

Except once again there was no escape. There were fences on both sides of this road as well, so all she could do was follow it. She didn't know where she was going, but she was sure that the farther she got from the truck, the better. That thought kept her going.

Looking around, she realized that the landscape was a little different from what she was used to. There were more trees. It was early spring so there were barely any leaves on them, but the trees were everywhere. Looking closer, she also realized that there were cattle near the trees, both steers and cows. There were no people around, but the cattle were in plain view.

"Hey," she called to them over the fence. "Who are you? What is this place?" A few of the animals raised their heads and looked over in her direction, but none of them moved. They just kept chewing their hay. "Hello," Emily called again, getting closer. "I said, who are you?"

"Who are you?" asked a large steer. Unlike most of the other cattle, who were brown and white like Emily, he was dark brown all over.

"Emily," she replied, approaching the fence that separated the road from the pasture where the cattle were. The steer moved toward her.

"Hello," he said calmly. He wasn't especially pleased to see her, but he wasn't unfriendly either. "I'm Orion."

"Hello," Emily replied. "What is this place? It looks nice."

"It is nice," Orion said. "It's where we live."

"Really?" Emily said, looking around. "You and the other cattle?"

"Yeah, and some dogs and horses as well."

"Horses?" Emily asked fearfully, remember the horses the cowboys had ridden on branding day. "You share this place with horses?"

"A few," Orion said. "But we don't have much to do with them. They pretty much keep to themselves. The dogs, too. They live in another part."

"Oh," Emily said. "That sounds okay...I guess." What was this place, she wondered, where cows, horses, and dogs lived side by side? It sounded too good to be true.

"Yeah, even the man who lives here is okay," Orion said.

"A man?" Emily asked. Now she knew it was too good to be true. She had had quite enough of men by now, no matter what Orion said about this one.

"Yeah, he gives us hay in the winter and brushes us and visits us from time to time. So do a couple of kids who come by."

Three people? Emily thought. What at first sounded like paradise was starting to sound like punishment. It seemed to her that the sooner she left it, the better. "That doesn't sound too good to me," she said to Orion.

"I know what you mean," he replied. "I didn't like people either, but this man and the children are different. There's one of them over there now. I think he was a little scared of us when he arrived, but he's okay now."

A boy was walking toward the main gate leading into the pasture. He didn't have a stick or an electric prod in his hand; he wasn't even wearing a cowboy hat. But that didn't fool Emily. She knew better. A human being was a human being, she told herself, and humans were bad news. "Well, I'm getting out of here," she said, eyeing the boy carefully.

"Why? I just told you he was okay," Orion said, although judging from his tone, Emily decided he probably didn't care much either way.

"I know, but I've just come from being pushed inside a box that was dark and filthy and frightening, and I don't want to go back to it or anything else like it."

"I don't blame you. I was in a box like that before I came here. But he wouldn't send you anywhere like that," Orion said, nodding at the boy. "He just lets you be. You'll see."

"Hey, Orion," the boy called, "who's your friend?"

Emily bristled. They boy was much nearer now, and she didn't like it. A few more steps and she'd have to run. Orion, however, turned toward the boy.

"What are you doing?" Emily asked in disbelief. How could Orion be so stupid? Didn't he know what people were like?

"He called me," Orion said. "And like I told you, he's a nice boy. We like him." With that, he turned away and walked toward the boy.

Emily watched, amazed. But Orion was right. When the boy reached Orion, he didn't hit him or scare him. He didn't do anything nasty to him. He just put his hand gently on Orion's forehead and stroked it. Emily didn't know what to do. She thought by now her little voice would have started telling her to run, but it was silent. So she just stood still and watched while Orion allowed the boy to stroke him over and over again.

"Hey, Chris," another human voice called from beyond the gate. "What are you doing?"

"Nothing," Chris said, "just saying hello to Orion. But there's a cow out there I don't recognize. I don't think I've ever seen her before."

"Hold on, I'll be right there," the second voice said.

Emily liked the sound of that voice even less. It was an older voice than the boy's, more like most of the human voices she was used to hearing on the range and in the feedlot, and it didn't have much kindness in it.

But still Orion didn't move. In fact, it wasn't long before a heifer came and joined him and the boy.

"Hello, Cumin," Chris said to the heifer, stroking her forehead, too. Cumin swished her tail calmly from one side to the other.

"Hey, you're right," the second voice said as it drew nearer. Emily could see now that it belonged to a large man like the biggest cowboys she'd seen on the ranch. Surely Orion knew better than to trust him. But Orion and Cumin stood still while he patted them and talked to the boy.

"I don't know where she came from," Chris said. "Have you seen her before?"

"No," said Mr. Bridges, "but we might as well see if we can get her inside. So she just sort of appeared from out of nowhere, did she?"

"I don't know," Chris said. "It sure looks like she did."

Both Chris and Mr. Bridges were still far enough away from Emily for her to feel safe. She knew from the way she outran the truck drivers that she could outrun these two people if she had to, but until they came closer, she felt it was okay to stand and watch what they did. It astonished her to see the way they treated Orion and Cumin, and she couldn't bear to take her eyes off them. However, as they passed through the gate and started to walk toward her, she grew more nervous. They didn't seem threatening in any way—instead, they called to her with very gentle voice, even the older man—but she still didn't like it. At any moment, she knew she would hear the little voice telling her to run. And when it did, she would be off like a shot.

"Hey, girl," Mr. Bridges called out tenderly. "Want some hay?" He was holding a bunch of it in his hand, and it looked very tasty to Emily. She hadn't had anything to eat in some time. "Come here, girl," he said.

Emily knew that at any second the little voice would tell her to run; it was simply a matter of time. And then she would be on her way again. Somewhere there had to be a place where she wouldn't have to deal with people anymore. In talking to Orion, she thought that this might be such a place, but now she knew better. The voice would tell her so at any moment.

Only it didn't. The man and boy walked closer and closer, and still the voice said nothing. What was wrong? Emily was confused. It had never let her down before. Clearly, the only thing to do, she decided, was act on her own. In fact, maybe that's what the voice's silence meant: that it was time she relied on her own judgment. And her judgment was telling her to bolt right...now!

Except at that moment when she was just about to turn on her hooves and flee for her life, a voice called out to her. Not the little voice inside her and not a human voice. It wasn't a voice she was expecting to hear ever again. It was Marigold's voice.

"Emily," Marigold called out to her. "Emily, is that really you?" As soon as Marigold had seen Emily, she wanted to believe it was her, but she wouldn't let herself. She knew from experience that once her children were taken away from her that she never saw them again, so there was no way this could be Emily, despite what sounded to her like Emily's voice. "No," she told herself, "it can't be her. It can't be. I mustn't allow myself to hope that it is."

But the closer she got and the more she looked, the more hopeful she became. Marigold moved a little closer. The voice sure did sound like Emily's, but surely she was kidding herself. She had to be. She was just allowing her hopes and imagination to run wild, and that was a mistake. Even so, there was something about the voice that made her move closer still.

Little by little she inched forward, telling herself with each step that she must be mistaken. It couldn't be Emily coming back to her. But then, just as Emily was about to run out of her life a second time, she knew she was right. It really was Emily standing in front of her.

"Emily," she called again, desperately this time. "It's your mother!"

Emily stopped and stared. She couldn't believe her eyes. It was Marigold. She had never stopped thinking about Marigold, not in all the time they had been parted. But she never thought she would see her again, not after what she had been through. Yet there she was. Her eyes weren't lying. It really was Marigold standing on the other side of the fence.

"Mother," Emily whispered, almost too shocked to speak. "I can't believe it."

"Neither can I," Marigold said. "Never in my wildest dreams..."

"Mother," Emily repeated. She was too overcome to know what to do or say.

"Come over to the other side of the fence," Marigold said. "Hurry. I want to see you better."

"I can't," Emily said. "I don't know how."

"Just follow the men," Marigold said. Mr. Bridges and Chris were quite near now, and Emily was certain she should run from them. But that would mean running from her mother, and she didn't want to do that. She didn't know what to do.

"But Mother, they're people," she said in a worried tone. "I can't go with them. They'll hurt me *and* you."

"They won't," Marigold said. "I promise. These people are different. Just follow them and they'll lead you to me."

"Follow them?" Emily was barely able to speak. This flew in the face of everything she knew and understood, everything she had learned. People were not to be trusted. It was a fact of life. Surely her mother knew that better than anyone. Yet here her mother was telling her to go with them.

"Go on," Marigold said, "follow them. I promise that you'll be okay."

"You promise?"

"I promise."

Emily looked at Marigold, at the stretch of road behind her, and at the two people gesturing at her with the hay. There was still time to run, and the road looked very tempting, but Marigold had promised. She was so close. All Emily had to do to be with her was get over that fence. If only these people could be trusted to take her there. If only...

"Okay," she finally said, as Chris and Mr. Bridges drew up to her. "Okay... I'll go with them."

Chapter Eleven

The Cow Boy

"*Hey, who have you got there?*" Gina called as Chris and Mr. Bridges led Emily through the gate and into the pasture. She had been so busy playing with the dogs that it was a while before she realized that her human companions had left her. "I've never seen her before."

"Neither have we," Chris said. "We found her on the road."

"She's got an *L* brand just like the one Mr. Bridges rescued from the auction last year," Gina said.

"Yeah, another one of Lansing's," Mr. Bridges said. "Hey, they seem to know each other."

No sooner was Emily through the gate than she ran over to Marigold. Mr. Bridges was amazed. His cattle usually got on well, but not as quickly as that.

"They must have known each other when they lived at Mr. Lansing's," Chris said.

"Maybe they did," Mr. Bridges said, still surprised. "I guess they're the only ones who'll ever know."

"I guess," Chris said.

"Oh well, all that matters now is that she's safe," Mr. Bridges continued. "We're going to have to call the Lansings to let them know we've got her."

"Call the Lansings?!" Gina cried. "Why do that? You're not going to give her back to them, are you? You can't. She belongs to you now."

"No, she doesn't," Mr. Bridges said. "We found her on the road, and she has the Lansing brand on her, so we've got to let them know in case they're missing her."

"But they'll just sell her for meat!" Gina yelled. "We can't let them do that."

"Gina, she doesn't belong to us," Mr. Bridges said. "This is a rescue ranch, not a hideout for cattle rustlers. I don't want the Lansings to sell her for meat either, but we've got to play by the rules."

"But...," Gina couldn't finish because at that moment the cell phone Mr. Bridges carried in his pocket began to ring.

"Hold on, Gina," he said, pulling out the aerial. "I'll talk to you about it in a minute.... Hello," he said into the phone. "No kiddin'," he said after a few minutes. "And it happened just today? Whaddyah know? Okay, I'll go over and take a look."

"What happened just today?" Chris asked when Mr. Bridges clicked off the phone.

"That was my brother," Mr. Bridges said. "He says a cattle truck had an accident on its way to the slaughterhouse. Its axle broke. A few animals were killed, and some more are badly injured. The news is all over town."

"Hey," Chris said excitedly. "That must be where the new cow came from. She must have escaped from the truck."

"Could be," Mr. Bridges said, heading toward his truck. "I'll find out when I get there."

"You see," Gina said, "it was on its way to the slaughterhouse. So they were going to kill her. You can't let that happen, Mr. Bridges."

"Gina, I'll see what I can do," Mr. Bridges said, getting into his truck. "But I told you before, we have to play by the rules. If she belongs to Mr. Lansing, we have to tell him we've got her. Then we'll see what happens. You know how people are about things like this."

"But…"

"Gina," Mr. Bridges said again, more sternly this time. "Just wait and see, okay?"

"Okay," Gina said, "but I'm not going to let her die. No way."

Mr. Bridges rolled up the window in his driver's door and put the truck in gear. Chris and Gina watched him drive away. "I can't believe he'd let anything happen to her," Gina said to Chris as they watched him go. "Not Mr. Bridges."

"Me neither," Chris said. "But remember what he said last week about not being able to rescue any more animals for a while? He said winter hay was really expensive this year, and he didn't have money to spend on more animals."

"But he took Alistair last week," Gina said. Alistair was an old dog Mr. Bridges had found shivering and starving behind a dumpster in town. He'd brought him home, warmed him, fed him, and then adopted him.

"But Alistair didn't belong to anybody," Chris said. "It seems the heifer does."

"But don't you want to save her?" Gina asked. "Don't you care if she goes to the slaughterhouse?"

Chris looked over to where Emily and Marigold were standing. In the months he'd been visiting the Rescue Ranch, he'd learned to like the cows and was glad that none of them would come to any harm. It was a nice idea. But he didn't care about them the way Gina did, and it still bothered him to hear her get so upset about things. It reminded him of why the other kids continued to think she was so strange.

"Well, don't you?" she asked again.

"Yeah, but…," Chris honestly didn't know what to say. He did care, only not as much as Gina did.

"Well, I do," Gina said, "and I'm going to save her."

"How?" Chris asked.

"If I have to, I'll buy her," Gina said. "I'll buy her from Mr. Lansing."

"But she could cost hundreds of dollars. Remember how much Mr. Bridges paid for Mr. Lansing's cow at the auction yard? I think it was over $800. You don't have $800, do you?"

"No, but I have $75 in my bank account. How much do you have?"

Wait a minute, Chris thought. He never said anything about giving Gina money to buy a cow. He was saving his money to buy a new program for his computer.

"Well?" Gina asked when Chris didn't answer. "Have you got any money?"

"Yes, about $45, but…"

Gina wouldn't let him finish. "So that's $120 right there," she said defiantly. She was so good at arithmetic that she could do the addition instantly in her head. "Only $680 to go."

"*Only* $680?" Chris said sarcastically. "It might as well be $680,000." And what made her think she could have his $45 anyway? He never said she could.

"You are such a pessimist," Gina said in a way that let Chris know she wouldn't give up. "I am going to raise the money, you'll see."

"How?" Chris asked, more annoyed than ever.

"I don't know," Gina admitted, "but I will. You'll see. Now let's go over and see my new cow. We've got to choose a name for her."

"Okay," Chris said. "But hey, since when is she *your* cow? I'm the one who found her."

"Okay, *our* cow," Gina said.

"That's better," Chris said. "*Our* cow."

Mr. Bridges returned after about an hour with more news of the accident. About eleven animals had died in it, he said, and many more had broken legs. They would have to be killed, too. "They were squashed so tight that they fell over each other," he said. "Those cattle trucks are wicked things. I wish someone would outlaw them."

"Me, too," Gina said.

Chris didn't say anything because he didn't know.

"But what about Esmeralda?" Gina asked. Esmeralda was the name she picked out for Emily. Chris wasn't sure about it.

"Who's Esmeralda?" Mr. Bridges asked.

"The new cow," Gina said. "That's what we named her."

"That's what *you* named her," Chris said. "I still think it's dumb. Esmeralda. It sounds like a witch's name." The business about his mom changing her name had taught him how important names were.

"No, it doesn't," Gina said. "I think it sounds mysterious, which is appropriate since Esmeralda's story is a mystery."

"Esmeralda, eh?" Mr. Bridges said. "I'm afraid I see Chris's point. It is a mouthful. What do you say we call her something else with an "E"? Say...I don't know...Emily maybe?"

"Emily," Gina said, horrified. "But that's so ordinary. I don't think she's an Emily at all."

"Okay, we'll compromise," Mr. Bridges said. "You call her Esmeralda, Gina, and Chris and I will call her Emily, and we'll all know what cow we're talking about. Besides, we might not have her much longer."

"What do you mean?" Gina asked. "Aren't we going to keep her?"

"John Lansing is coming over tomorrow to have a look at her," Mr. Bridges said. "He wants to see if she's his. She also might belong to Jim Shank since it was his cattle who were being transported in the truck. Anyway, we have to find out."

"But why?" Gina asked. "Why not just keep her?"

"I told you before, Gina. We can't steal cows. People criticize me enough for what I do without thinking I'm a thief, too. And I'm not going to give them any more ammunition to use against me."

"Well, it doesn't matter," Gina said, "because Chris and I have decided we're going to buy her for you."

"What!" Chris yelled. "I never said that. Who said I was going to buy her?"

"I thought we agreed," Gina said. "We have $120 between us, so we have to raise the rest of the money we need to buy her."

"You two?" Mr. Bridges said. "Well, that would be great because you know I don't have the money right now to buy her myself. I wish I had because Emily's a beautiful animal, and I sure don't want to see anything happen to her."

"Then it's settled," Gina said proudly.

"No, it isn't," said Chris. "You still don't have the money. You've got to raise it, remember?"

"I remember," Gina said, "and I will. I'll ask the kids at school if they want to help."

"The kids at school?!" Chris shouted. Was she out of her mind? "You gotta be kidding! They're not going to help you! They think you're a freak for believing all this stuff in the first place! They're all ranchers, remember? They all eat cows! They'll just laugh you out of the building!"

Gina said nothing. It looked as if she might cry at first, but then she calmed down. She stiffened her lip, looked away from Chris, and turned to go.

"Gina, I didn't mean that," Chris said. He felt terrible now for saying that the other kids thought she was a freak. He knew she knew it herself, but that was still no reason for him to say it. If only she hadn't made him so angry.

Gina still said nothing and got on her bike.

"Gina?" Chris said again as she began to ride away. "Gina? Come back, Gina, okay?"

"Just let her go," Mr. Bridges said as they watched her. "She gets this way sometimes."

"I know," Chris said. It wasn't as if he hadn't seen it before. "And I really like her—most of the time—but she makes me so mad sometimes. She gets so upset about things."

"The way I do?" Mr. Bridges said.

"Oh, I don't know," Chris said, a little embarrassed. "I didn't mean that."

"I know you didn't," Mr. Bridges said more kindly. Then he put an arm around Chris's shoulder. "Don't worry about it. Go home and we'll figure out Emily's future tomorrow. She'll be fine tonight. At least you can be sure of that."

"Okay," Chris said, but he still felt terrible. The day sure hadn't gone the way he hoped it would, and the next day, he worried, might be even worse.

"So, how was the ranch?" Helene asked Chris when he got home. "Did you have fun today?"

It was the wrong question. Chris was so upset, he scarcely knew where to begin. He waved his arms, stamped his feet, shook his head, and wished as hard as he could that the whole thing had never happened. Except it had.

"Calm down," Helene said, going over to him. "Nothing can be that bad. Now sit down and tell me what happened. I'm sure we can work something out."

Chris wasn't so sure, but he told her anyway. He told her all about Emily and Gina and Mr. Bridges, and how Gina was planning to spend his money buying Emily even though he hadn't given her permission, and how he didn't know how he was going to get out of it or even if he should. All he wanted was to die.

"Of course, you don't want to die," Helene said. "But I understand why you're upset. The main question is: Do you want to help her buy the cow?"

"I don't know," Chris said, still shaking his head. "I was sorta saving up to buy a computer program, not a cow. But Gina looked so sad when she rode away, and I do kinda like Emily. I guess. I think. Oh, I don't know. I just wish..." But he didn't really know what he wished.

"Look, dinner's almost ready," Helene said. "What do you say you go upstairs, get washed, and then have something to eat? I think you'll feel better after that."

Chris didn't think he'd ever feel better again, but what choice did he have? He might as well do what she suggested. "What are we having?" he asked, as he started climbing the stairs. "Not beef, I hope."

"No," Helene laughed, "not beef."

"Well, that's something at least," Chris said, hanging his head as he headed toward his room.

"What was that all about?" Andrew asked as Chris disappeared upstairs. "What's Chris so upset about?"

Helene told him.

"A cow?" Andrew said, shaking his head in disbelief. "What does he want with a cow? The country's full of cows. Hasn't he noticed?"

"Shhh, don't upset him," Helene said when Chris reappeared. "I told him we wouldn't talk about it over dinner."

"Buy a cow," Andrew muttered under his breath. "I never heard anything so silly. City kids."

After dinner, Chris went upstairs to play video games on the computer, while his mother phoned Sylvia Lansing.

It was the second time they spoke that day. Sylvia had come around to visit earlier, with a new blend of coffee and the same old problem—her husband.

"John doesn't seem to understand that when I want to try new things—things that he might not enjoy—that I'm not saying I don't love him," she told Helene over a plate of almond cookies that Helene had baked. "I just want to be free to try these things without him disapproving or thinking they're some kind of threat to him."

"I don't think there's anything wrong with that," Helene said, enjoying the coffee. "Everybody likes different things. Look at Andrew and me. He loves that wretched rodeo of his, and I couldn't stand it."

"It is awful, isn't it?" interrupted Sylvia.

"Terrible," Helene replied. "But just because he likes it and I hate it doesn't mean I hate him. I'm still in love with him, and he knows it."

"The worst thing is that the more John disapproves, the more dif-

ferent I want to be. Sometimes I think I want to do something really
... I don't know, something almost crazy just to force him to wake up
and realize that change isn't always something to be frightened of.
Sometimes it's fun and exciting and even for the best."

"What kind of thing?" Helene asked, biting into a cookie.

"I don't know. I haven't decided. I just have this feeling that one
day something will happen, and when it does I'll want to..."

"Pounce?" offered Helene.

"Yes, pounce," replied Sylvia. They both laughed.

The memory of that conversation made Helene smile as she
phoned Sylvia to ask if she knew if Emily belonged to John.

"I couldn't tell you," Sylvia said. "We have so many. John buys
and sells so many that I'm surprised he can keep track of them. But
if she has our brand, she must have been ours at one time."

"Do you think John will want her back?" Helene asked.

"If she's his, yes," Sylvia said. "But you say Chris wants to buy
her?"

"I don't know," Helene said. "Neither does he. His friend, Gina,
the one who's so into animals, is all hot and bothered about it. She's
determined to raise the money and she wants Chris to help her. But
Chris is just confused."

"Poor boy," Mrs. Lansing said. "It's so hard to know what to do
under these circumstances, isn't it?"

"It sure is," Helene said. "I like the fact that he cares so much, but
this is a ranching community. You're a rancher yourself."

"Please, Helene, John is a rancher. I'm a rancher's wife."

"Okay, a rancher's wife," Helene corrected herself. "But you
make your money buying and selling cattle. So who's to say you're
wrong? Who's to say Emily, or whatever her name is, shouldn't go
back to the feedlot or on to the slaughterhouse or wherever it is she
belongs?"

Mrs. Lansing didn't reply. For a moment Helene thought the
phone had gone dead. "Sylvia, are you there? Sylvia?" She shook the
receiver and knocked it against her hand. "Sylvia?"

"Oh...sorry," Mrs. Lansing finally replied. "I...ah...sorry. Yes, I'm still here. I was just thinking about what you said and what we were talking about this afternoon. Tell you what, I've got to go now, but I'll talk to you again tomorrow. In fact, I might just go over to the Rescue Ranch and see Emily myself."

"Oh, would you?" Helene enthused. "That would be marvelous. I'm sure it would make Chris feel better if you were there."

"I'll do my best," Sylvia said. "And tell Chris not to worry."

"Easier said than done," Helene said, "but I will."

The next day a whole group of people arrived at the Rescue Ranch to look at Emily. There was Gina, Chris, Sylvia and John Lansing, Ted Lansing, and Jim Shank.

"She's mine, all right," Mr. Shank said. "I bought her from you and Ted at auction last fall," he said to Mr. Lansing. "A panel door broke open in the accident, and she musta got out of it."

"Okay," Mr. Lansing said, already bored with the whole business. "That's fine with me." All he wanted was to get back to his ranch and not waste any more time on one lost heifer that wasn't even his anymore. "Sorry to take up your time, Mr. Bridges. And thanks for looking after things."

"Right, so I'll take her in the truck," Mr. Shank said, gesturing at a smaller transport truck he'd driven to the ranch. "I lost a lot o' money in that accident, and I can't afford to lose any more."

"Wait!" Gina shouted. "You can't take her because I'm going to buy her."

"You?" Mr. Shank said. "You're gonna buy that heifer? What for?"

"To save her life," Gina declared.

Mr. Shank and Ted started to laugh, but Gina looked so hurt that they stopped almost as soon as they started. "Listen, Gina," Mr. Shank continued, looking as serious as he could. "It is Gina, right?"

"Yes," Gina said.

"You're a good kid, but that cow belongs to me. She's worth a lot o' money to me. That's how I make my living, buying and selling animals like her. So if you really want her, it's gonna cost you $1,200."

"Twelve hundred?" Gina cried. "I thought she would cost $800. Why $1,200?"

"'Cause that's what she's worth to me," Mr. Shank said. "And like I said, I lost a lot o' money in that accident—a lot o' animals I coulda sold for slaughter were killed—and I gotta make some of it back somehow."

"Okay, then, $1,200," Gina said. "I don't have the money now, but I'll get it for you. Here's $75 to start. I took it out of the bank this morning. It's as much as I have right now." She took the money out of her pocket and handed it to Mr. Shank.

"Seventy-five," Mr. Shank said. "Listen, Gina, I need twelve hundred bucks for that cow, not a cent less. And I can't wait for the rest. So either you give it to me now, or you don't get the cow."

"But I told you, I don't have it now," Gina explained in frustration. "I'll get it as quickly as I can though. Just give me some time."

"I've got $45," Chris said.

"Chris?!" Gina said. She had barely looked at him until now, but now she was staring at him in disbelief. "I didn't think..."

"I said, I've got $45," Chris continued. Seeing Gina stand up to Mr. Shank so bravely had finally helped him make up his mind. If she believed in something enough to risk becoming a laughingstock to a whole school and a whole town, then the least he could do was help. He knew it wouldn't be easy, but letting Gina down would be even harder. Suddenly, it all seemed so clear. He couldn't understand why it had taken him so long to see it. But now that he knew what he wanted, he felt great. In fact, he hadn't felt this free since he left the city. "It's in the bank," he said to Mr. Shank, "but I can get it for you today."

"Listen, kids," Mr. Shank replied, getting a little impatient. "Seventy-five, forty-five, it isn't enough. Don't you understand? She's worth $1,200, and I can get that for her right now at Smith's." Smith's, a slaughterhouse, was only a few miles down the road.

"But I told you I'd get it for you," Gina said. "Just give me a few days. That's all it'll take, I promise."

"I'll help her," Chris said. "We'll ask our parents and the kids at school and..."

"The kids at school!" Gina repeated. She had a look of real wonder on her face. "I thought you said..."

"Yeah, the kids at school," Chris said again, as if it were the most logical idea in the world. Suddenly, despite everything, it was. "We'll..."

"Kids, for the last time, save your breath," Mr. Shank interrupted. He looked as if he was about to explode. "If you want an animal, get yourselves a dog, okay? Although, maybe you got enough o' those around here already." Mr. Bridges's dogs had barked up a storm when he arrived, and had jumped all over him. "But that heifer is comin' with me."

"Mr. Bridges," Gina appealed, "can't you...?"

"Listen, Shank," Mr. Bridges said, "I don't have the money either. At least not now. We've had a lot o' expenses around here lately, but gimme a few weeks, and like Gina said, we'll get you the money. Just give us time."

"Doesn't anybody here understand?" Mr. Shank shouted. "I need the money now. Not tomorrow, not the next day, not the day after that. *Now!* So either you got the money now, or I take the cow away with me. Got it?"

"I understand," Mrs. Lansing said. She hadn't spoken until now, but she had been listening carefully to everything that had been said.

"Sylvia," Mr. Lansing said, "don't get mixed up in this. We have to get home. I'm busy, and I've wasted enough time with all this."

"Fine," she said, "I'll be with you in a minute. But first I've got to finish this."

"Finish what?" Mr. Lansing asked, rolling his eyes with exasperation. "There's nothing to finish. It's Jim's cow, not ours. He bought it from Ted at auction, right Ted?"

"Right," Ted said, although if he were completely honest, he would have admitted that if it hadn't been for the *L* brand on Emily's flank, he wouldn't have known her from a thousand other animals.

"I know," Mrs. Lansing said calmly. "That's why I'm going to buy her from Mr. Shank."

"What?!" John and Ted Lansing shouted in unison. "Are you crazy?" John said.

"Yeah, are you crazy?" Ted echoed.

"Sylvia," Mr. Lansing continued, "we don't want her. That's why we sold her. She's no good to us, so you can't buy her back."

"I understand that," Mrs. Lansing said. "I'm not buying her for us. I'm buying her for Mr. Bridges and Chris and Gina. But most of all, I'm buying her for herself."

"For herself?" Mr. Lansing yelled. "What on earth are you talking about?" He was flabbergasted. "Have you lost your mind? You think a cow understands $1,200?"

"Of course not," Mrs. Lansing said, pulling her checkbook out of her purse. "But that's not the point. It never was. Mr. Shank, to whom should I make out this check?"

Mr. Shank thought the whole thing was a great joke, and was glad that his own wife hadn't gone off the deep end the way Mrs. Lansing evidently had. But he didn't care where the money came from, as long as he got it. "Make it out to me," he said, laughing, "and the cow's all yours."

"No," Mrs. Lansing said, making out the check, "the cow is all hers."

"Whose?" Chris asked. "Gina's?"

"No," Gina said, "not mine. I think what Mrs. Lansing means is that Esmeralda belongs to herself."

"Emily," Chris corrected her.

Mrs. Lansing just smiled. She didn't need to say anything more; Gina understood perfectly.

"Well, one thing's for sure, she ain't mine anymore," Mr. Shank said, snapping up the check. "Good-bye everyone. Nice doin' business with ya."

"Good-bye," Mrs. Lansing said.

"Good-bye, good-bye," Gina, Chris, and Mr. Bridges added. Mr. Lansing just shook his head.

"I sure do want to thank you," Mr. Bridges said to Mrs. Lansing, holding out his hand to her. "That was a very nice thing you did. I know the kids appreciate it. And it makes me think that maybe I've misjudged a few people around here. Maybe I should start looking at them in a different way."

"It was my pleasure," Mrs. Lansing said. "But you're the one I should be thanking. You're the one who started all this." She gestured around at the ranch.

"Well, I don't know about that," Mr. Bridges said, "but I do know I learned a thing or two today."

"So did I," Chris added.

"So did I," Gina said, smiling at him.

Only Ted and Mr. Lansing said nothing. They were too disgusted.

After a few minutes Gina said. "Say, Chris, you wanna go and tell Esmeralda the good news?"

"Okay," Chris said, running after her. "Except her name is Emily! You got that, Gina? It's Emily!"

Happily Ever After?

*N*ow that it was summer, the trees were heavy with leaves, and they formed a lush, green canopy over the ground. When the sun got too hot, as it often did at midday, Emily stood under them. They were so thick in places that they almost made the sun disappear. She especially liked it when a breeze pushed a low-lying branch along her back and over her head so that for a moment the only things she could see were the leaves' green outlines silhouetted against the light.

She wasn't afraid of anything now. Over time she had learned that Orion was right, that Chris, Gina, and Mr. Bridges were there only to help, never to hurt. She wasn't even bothered by Mr. Bridges's truck. He could drive it right up to her in the pasture. Sometimes she wouldn't even turn around when she heard its engine. It depended on whether she was thinking about something else.

Marigold was always nearby, and she had new friends to keep her company as well. Like her, all of them had been in some kind of trouble, but in the end, they had been lucky enough to be rescued by Mr. Bridges. None of them knew why, but all of them were grateful.

Marigold explained to Emily about how Mr. Bridges had bought her at auction. She said she had been heartbroken to leave Paige and Cinnamon, and terrified when, like Emily and so many of her other calves, she had been loaded onto a truck for an unknown destination. But in the end, it had been all right when Mr. Bridges brought her to the ranch.

"Even now, I sometimes can't believe it," Marigold said to Emily on a particularly sunny day when all the cows were huddled under the trees for shade. "And then when I think about how you escaped from that truck... Well, it's almost too much for me to take in."

Emily nodded, but the truth was she didn't think about things the way her mother did. Marigold believed everything was left to chance, and that somehow good fortune had smiled on both of them. Emily believed in good fortune, too, but she also believed in herself. After all, she was the one that had run from the truck. She had promised herself long ago that she would be different from all the other cows, and now here she was, proof of it.

"Remember how when you were small and we were on the range together, you said you never wanted to leave it?" Marigold said.

"I remember," Emily replied.

"I didn't like hearing you say such things then because I'd seen so many of my other calves leave the range. I didn't want you to harbor any false hopes. But if you were to say the same thing about this place, I wouldn't mind at all because I believe the same thing. I never want to leave here, and I'm sure you don't either. I'm sure you've had enough adventures to last a lifetime."

Emily allowed a low-lying branch to massage her back and head. It felt so good—so soft and yet so wonderfully alive.

"Emily?" Marigold asked. "Did you hear me? I said I'm sure you've had enough adventures to last a lifetime."

Emily walked out into the sunlight and lifted her face into it. The sun was very hot, but she didn't mind. When it became uncomfortable, she could always return to the shade. It was her choice.

"Emily," Marigold said again. "Are you listening to me?"

"Yes," Emily said, "You said I've had enough adventures to last a lifetime."

"That's right," Marigold said. "Sometimes you drift so far away that I wonder if you even hear me."

"I do," Emily said.

"So, am I right?" Marigold continued. "Haven't you had enough adventures by now?"

Emily shut her eyes and lifted her head toward the sun again. It felt really good today for some reason, not too hot at all.

"Well?" Marigold asked again. "Emily?...Emily?"